In Pain on Purpose

in Pain on Purpose

Donita J. Clark

Printed in the United States of America

Dedication

This book is dedicated to some young woman or man, struggling with the events in their life. My hope is to bring some young person reading this, peace with your past, and guidance for your future. A glimmer of hope in the midst of your pain.

Acknowledgements

I would like to thank my husband for supporting me in all of my endeavors, and loving me unconditionally.

A special thank you to my sister, Helen Allen, for always supporting me and lending me a spiritual word.

A special thank you to my daughter, Quanteisha Clark, for always being a sounding board and a voice of reason.

I would like to thank all of those that inspired me to write this book.

And last, but not least, thank you, Mr. Dawson, for always believing in me!

Preface

I spent many years of my life judging myself for my outward appearance. I watched tv or reality shows fantasizing about being a slimmer, prettier, more glamorous me. The truth is, I wasn't ugly on the outside but damaged on the inside.

It took many years and many relationships for me to realize that I was worth more than gold. I had surrounded myself with people that had no purpose. They lacked any real insight into life. Surrounding myself with other individuals who lacked the very foundation that I sought to gain would never change my mindset or my heart. The heart of a person controls their thinking, their beliefs, and moral reasoning.

Annie was my mother by definition; she lacked the gift of parental guidance and motherly affection. Annie displayed the misguided love of a mother. She was known in the streets as Queen. She ran drugs for all the b-boys in the neighborhood. She had a gift for hustling, and they knew she would do anything to feed her habit. Hank was the gangsta love of my life. He was bold, arrogant, and confident. He took what he wanted, from whoever he wanted, including me. Hank was the most selfish, inconsiderate man I have ever loved! My relationships with Hank and Annie can best be described as a journey through hell and back, twice!

Allow me to introduce myself; my name is Nyla. I am a young woman who has experienced more in my short years of life, than a 70-year old woman. As I lie here, in this hollow grave, I can't help but reminisce on the painful events of my past. So many memories flow in and out of my mind like short movie clips.

The memories flow through my mind so vividly I can feel my heart racing. The memories take me back to the most painful times in my life. The hurt and pain of my past felt all too real. It was as if I was experiencing each moment for the very first time. At the age of three, I can remember my father setting our house on fire. As our home burned to the ground, I can recall my mother running around in a panic. She tried to gather my sister and I as the flames raced toward the furniture. Dark, thick smoke filled the room as the burning items were engulfed in flames. You could hear the sounds of sirens from afar. My mother held us tight in her arms as tears rolled down her face. We stood outside of the apartment building as the flames grew thicker and larger. The flames seemed to be growing out of control. When the firefighters arrived on the scene, the fire had spread through three-quarters of the single level, single file, apartments. A firefighter rushed into the building to save a screaming woman. She had been trapped in the bathroom with her young child.

At the age of 11, I encountered a man that stole my innocence. Molestation can create negative imagery of one's self. It steals your self-esteem, your worth, and your purpose. A thoughtless act can change the entire course of your destiny. The victim is left with the shame and guilt of what happened, leaving their existence in question; a residue of hopeless decisions with endless consequences. At the age of 14, my mother was sent to prison for a manslaughter conviction. Later that year, I gave birth to my first child. My child was born out of the need to feel unconditional love and acceptance. At the age of 16, I was engaged for the first time. He loved the beautiful woman he saw inside of me, but I couldn't see her for myself. At the age of 17, I had my second child. At the age of 19, I graduated from high school. At the age of 20, I got married for the first time.

This seems like a simple progression of events, but nothing about my life has been simple. I wondered if this was the end of my life or the beginning of my future.

Chapter 1 - Being ME

People have always looked at my life and judged it. You look too serious, you don't have enough education, you have too many children, and of course, you're too loud and too outspoken. The events of my life have changed my perception of people and those who I allow into my inner circle. As I lie here, staring at the sky from this hollow grave, I reflect on the decisions I have made. Was I a reflection of the traumatic events that had occurred in my life? I spent years trying to get out from under the shadow of shame and guilt. It was embedded in every decision I had ever made.

I was born in Wooster, Ohio, on February 10, 1976. The year 1976 was considered the centennial year. Ohio had experienced the longest warm spell, from February 9th through the 23rd, lasting 15 consecutive days. February is typically one of the coldest months of the year, so this was unusual.

I am the daughter of Imus and Annie. My mother was 17-years old when she gave birth to me. She was a short woman, 5' 4" tall, mocha colored, high cheek bones, thin waist, big breasts, and hair that hung to her shoulders. She was raised by the men in her life, which means, they didn't spend a lot of money on cosmetic things like clothes or upkeep. Annie grew up on the poorer side of town. She was from a small town where they spent their Friday nights at high school football games. There wasn't much to do for young teenagers.

My father was 19-years old when I was born. I've heard several variations of the story, but they amount to the same dysfunction. Annie was a troubled girl in her youth. Her lack of structure led her into mischief and mayhem. With no close relatives, she went to live with her two uncles, her father's brothers. Both of her parents were killed in a home invasion when she was seven-years-old. She watched from the closet as they were brutally beaten then violently stabbed to death by two young men. Uncle Slick was a street pimp, and Uncle Sly was the manager at a strip club. Uncle Slick brought the girls in from the street, and Uncle Sly made sure they were able to entertain the men in the club.

My grandfather, GP, was the biggest pimp of them all. He once threw a woman off a building because she married one of her johns. He needed to prove to all the other women, including my grandmother, he meant business. The woman died after landing on the pavement from five stories up. My grandmother stood there shaking with fear. She knew that my grandfather was capable of anything.

A year and a half later, Sally, one of GP's girls, came home from a long night of working and found GP and my grandmother, Elizabeth, dead. The two of them were found in the bedroom. GP had been stabbed 28 times, and Elizabeth had her throat slashed. Elizabeth died quickly, but GP was stabbed and beaten repeatedly. Elizabeth was not the target of the rage.

Rumors say that one of the working girls paid two young boys to get their revenge. The girls held a grudge against GP for throwing the young woman off the building. The two young men disappeared, and the police never arrested anyone for my grandparent's murder.

Annie was seven-years-old when she was removed from her home. She sat in the closet and didn't move while the intruders viciously murdered her parents. When the police arrived, they searched the home. When the detectives opened the door, they found Annie balled up. She had a paralyzing look of fear on her face. The officers tried to shield her from the grotesque images, but she had already heard too much. The images of the grotesque beating had severe repercussions on Annie's life.

In the 1960s, there were no counseling sessions for children of a lower economic status. People moved on and buried their feelings.

My father, Imus, was a first-year college student when they met. Annie was in high school. He was studying to become a business manager. He was an attractive man, tall, thin, chocolate complexion with a short afro. He had a calm and cool swag that attracted the ladies. Women loved that he was smart, educated, and came from a good family. My paternal grandparents owned a neighborhood dry cleaner and laundromat. It was family owned and operated. Imus worked at the dry cleaners in the evenings after school and on the weekends.

He worked hard to help his family run the businesses. He had dreams of graduating from college and moving to the big city. He didn't care what city, he just wanted to get out of the little country town they lived in. The city was small enough that everyone knew everyone. Anything that happened made city news before you could get home to tell your parents. My grandparents enjoyed living the quiet, country life but Imus didn't. He wanted to travel the world. He knew that there was something far greater for him out there. He could only dream of his future possibilities.

Imus was 19-years old, and Annie was 17-years old when they began having children. Imus and Annie's relationship began as a whirlwind love affair. The romance began to dwindle once they began to have children. The responsibility of adulthood was all too surreal. They constantly fought about the neglect my sister, and I experienced. Imus wanted to know why Annie wouldn't grow up and take responsibility for her children. Eventually, the fighting while they were together, led to fighting while they were apart. These stories have mesmerized me from the beginning.

Especially when you hear the detailed accounts of your life from family members who recall these times. Annie told me the story of my grandparents when I was a child. I always wanted to know why I hadn't met them. Imus's sister, Yolanda, was the historian for his side of the family. She and Annie were close friends when she and Imus dated. The sad part about these stories is there's no beginning. I have never heard the beginning, only the end.

Annie dropped me off, at five-months-old, at a stranger's house with a promise to return for me. Annie was on the run because she and her friends had robbed the local convenience store. Annie knew a number of people who she called family. She wasn't very close with her biological family, so she adopted the people she hung around with. She always had an aunt or uncle who she could call on. Annie knew she was a wanted fugitive so she had to leave me with someone who would protect me.

When Imus found out that Annie left me with strangers, he demanded that she return me to him. Annie assured him that I was safe, but Imus didn't trust her. Annie said that she would be in touch with Imus the following day, but instead, the police showed up at his front door. Two officers knocked on the door the following morning with me wrapped in a pink baby blanket. They asked Imus to show them some I.D. They said that they had arrested Annie at a friend's house and she asked that I be returned to him. She was arrested for conspiracy to commit robbery. They hadn't stolen anything but some donuts and petty cash. The judge let Annie go because she was a young woman with a baby of her own. It was a small town; I suspect that the judge knew her uncles. Never heard what happened to her two friends.

Imus and Annie had two children within a two-year time span. When I was five-months-old Annie was already pregnant with my younger sister. Annie gave birth to her second daughter nine months later. My younger sister, Jasmine, is only 14 months younger than I. She was born the following April of 1977. Now, Imus and Annie had two children to care for. Imus understood the advantages of growing up in a two-parent, loving home and he wanted to provide the same stability for his children. He had accepted responsibility for his children and he wanted to be a loving parent.

He worked hard to try and keep his family together. He loved Annie but had no idea what she had gone through as a child. He was in love with the person he thought she was. He didn't know who she truly was or what she had been through. She hid her past in order to start a future with him. Imus would quickly find out all the things that she was trying to hide. It didn't matter what she was trying to hide on the outside; her truth was buried deep within. People think that if you don't speak your truth that it doesn't show. It's quite the opposite. Imus and

Annie could not reconcile their differences, so Annie decided to move on.

Annie was walking down the street wearing a pair of white pants that hugged her body. They accentuated every curve. She was a short woman, with a large chest. She had high cheek bones and a beautiful smile. A man pulled up alongside her playing an Al Green song on the radio. She stopped and smiled as he asked for her number. He asked if he could give her a ride to her destination. She was only around the corner from her house, so she pointed and smiled. She answered him saying she lived right over there. He asked if he could take her out on a date sometime. She was flattered at the invitation, so she said yes. They made plans to meet later that week for dinner. They exchanged numbers, and she walked away with a huge grin on her face.

Friday came, and it was date night. Clay arrived at her house about 7:00 p.m. He blew the horn and Annie opened the door. She was dressed in a short black mini skirt and multi-colored halter top. She had on tall black heels and small gold earrings. She had fresh curls in her hair, and it flowed as the wind blew. She walked to the car in slow motion so Clay could take in her appearance.

Clay stood outside the car holding the car door open. He was mesmerized by her beauty. Clay drove a long old-school car with leather seats. She got in the car, and he closed the door behind her. They drove to a restaurant that was about a mile from her home. They arrived at a restaurant decorated in authentic Chinese décor. Upon entering the restaurant, they were greeted by waiters and waitresses dressed in authentic Chinese attire. Annie was impressed by what she had seen so far. Clay and Annie talked for hours over dinner; they connected right away.

Clay was in his mid-thirties. A more distinguished gentleman, he was divorced and had two children. He showed true interest in Annie. He was willing and ready to take care of her and her children. She believed she had found someone who accepted the person she desired to be.

Clay and Annie's relationship developed quickly. Imus still wanted to work things out, but Annie refused him. With a new man in the picture, Imus posed a threat to their relationship. Annie told Imus that she was no longer interested in him. She was involved with someone else and felt it would be best if they both moved on. Imus wasn't entirely innocent in all this; he had his share of girls in high school. He was a nice looking man who came from a good background. He dated his share of women, but no one like Annie. She was special to him, and he would do anything to change how she felt about him. He wanted to win her love back.

Annie told Clay that Imus was still interested in her. Clay and Annie decided that Imus needed to be removed from the picture. They devised a plan that would get rid of him. Clay told Annie to invite Imus over. Annie called Imus and told him to come over for a talk. Imus smiled with anticipation and hung up the phone. He believed that she wanted to get back together. After all, they had a family to raise.

Imus came right over. He got to Annie's house and knocked on the door. She opened the door with a big smile on her face. She stepped aside and welcomed him into the house. Jasmine and I were in the living room watching cartoons. When the door opened, Imus entered, we got up and ran to him. He was standing in the middle of the floor with open arms. As Imus was engaged with the children, he didn't notice Annie's absence. While he was sitting in the living room playing with the children, Annie snuck out the back door. She went to the phone booth on the corner to call the police. As they sat in the living room, they heard deep banging on the door. The banging startled them all. They paused and looked at one another. He was hesitant about opening the door.

An uncertain Imus called out, "Who is it?"

A deep voice replied, "Open the door Mr. Y. It's the police!"

Imus got up and moved toward the door slowly. He opened the door slowly, unsure who was on the other side.

As he opened the door, the officers yelled out, "Put your hands up! Step back sir and place your hands behind your back!"

He looked puzzled as the police told him to place his hands behind his back. Imus questioned, "What is this about?"

The police stated, "You're under arrest for arson!"

"Arson?" He asked.

The police officer replied, "Annie has filed a report stating that you started the fire at her last residence. She also stated that you threatened to hurt her and take her children."

Imus looked confused. He shouted, "Wait, wait, wait! Annie said that I could come over and see the girls!"

We watched as he was pulled out the door and placed into the back of the police car. Annie stood behind the officers until Imus was placed in the car. You could hear him yelling from the back seat, "Annie, why are you doing this to me? I haven't done anything wrong! I'm sorry Annie! Please, forgive me!" The pleas and screams wouldn't change her mind. She wanted to move on with her life in the best way she knew how.

Clay had set things in motion and waited at home to hear from Annie. Annie called Clay and told him that their plan had been successful. Annie knew that Imus' family would eventually be coming to question her, so she packed her bags and went to stay with Clay. I can remember her placing us in the car in the middle of the night. Annie decided that she was going to move in with Clay. He had his own home, and he welcomed us. Clay was known around town so they decided that they'd move away. It was a small town and news traveled fast.

Annie took us before my grandparents could get word of Imus' arrest. He had been arrested but hadn't had time to make his first phone call. It would be several hours before the booking process was complete. We didn't hear what happened until years later. We were around the ages of three and four years old when this all happened. He was tried and sentenced to two years in prison. After his release, he moved back to his home state of South Carolina. We lost contact with him after that night. We could not have imagined that it would be 30 years before we laid eyes on him again.

Annie and Clay....

Annie and Clay had kept their romance a secret, but they couldn't hide it for long. Once Annie moved in with Clay, she would quickly realize that he was short tempered and very abusive. He liked his home kept a certain way. He believed that women should tend to the home and the children.

Annie had been raised by men, but she didn't take kindly to orders. Annie found out very quickly why Clay had been divorced. The fights began over the simplest things. As time went on, they escalated into broken jaws and cracked ribs. Clay would bring us to the hospital to visit her after their violent fights. He would bring her flowers and confess how much he loved her. I used to wonder why he would be the one bringing her flowers when he inflicted the injuries.

While Annie was in the hospital being treated for her injuries, she found out that she was pregnant by Clay. They were expecting their first child. She would surely take him back now that they were starting a family together.

Clay wasn't a new father; he had two children from his previous marriage. This was their first child together.

It's hard to describe my childhood because there were so many traumatic events.

Most of the situations are circumstances that most people never encounter. Some people are fortunate enough to only read these stories in books or see in movies. For some individuals, these are situations that happen on an everyday occurrence. I feel that when I try to share my experiences, people look at me and stare.

Chapter 2 -
Enduring Abuse

Clay and Annie packed up the Cadillac and moved across the country to Minnesota. Annie had left her family behind. She was in love with this man and planned to start a future together. She had forgiven him for breaking her jaw. He explained that it was an accident. Things had gotten out of control, and she just pushed him too far. As long as he apologized for what he did, they would move on.

In the first five months that we lived in Minnesota, Annie gave birth to her first son, Iman. He was born in March of 1982. He was a special little being to me. I cuddled with him like he was a doll. He was six years younger than me, and I loved everything about him.

When we first arrived in Minnesota, we spent several months living with Clay's family. The transition was hard for Annie because she had to endure all the tension from Clay's family. Clay's mother despised Annie and her children. She did everything she could to make Annie feel uncomfortable. Annie told Clay that they needed to find their own apartment quickly. She respected his mother but didn't want to live in a hostile environment with her newborn baby and young children.

Clay was a middle child, but he was favored by his mother. She was excited to have him in her home but regretted the company he brought along. It was quite easy for Clay to establish his life here. He quickly got a job as a cab driver. Learning his way around the city came with the territory. He met people from all walks of life in his job. Networking with his clients opened up a number of legal and illegal resources. His job combined with his family connections, aided in their transition.

In his travels, he met a man who managed a number of rental properties in the surrounding suburbs. He explained his situation to the gentleman, and they connected from there. Clay knew that Annie wasn't comfortable living with his family so he wanted to find a place that they could call home. Their plans were to stay with family until they could save enough money to move into their own place.

Nate, the property manager Clay met in his cab, agreed to show him a rental home in Burnsville. Burnsville was a very nice suburb of Minneapolis. The suburb was quiet and had little to no crime. The townhome was a 30-minute drive from the city.

Clay and Annie took the three of us to view the townhouse with them. When we pulled into the subdivision, Annie immediately fell in love with the community. There were clusters of brown townhomes to the right and left of the entrance. The grass was thick green and healthy throughout the community. We drove down the street to the second cluster of homes. We took a right turn and then a left before arriving at the cul-de-sac.

Our townhouse was the last one on the left-hand side. There were two units on each side of the driveway. We pulled into the driveway and got out of the car. I looked around to see if there were any signs of children. There were no children outside anywhere. We walked to the bottom of the stairs, and Annie looked back to make sure we were behind her. As we entered the house, Clay and Annie went upstairs with the property manager and we went downstairs. We knew to be quiet and behave ourselves while the grownups were talking. The townhouse was a split-level. We walked around downstairs and noticed two doors, one on each wall. We opened the one to the left first. It led out to the garage. The one to the right led into a family room. The family room had a wall with a fireplace. There was also another bedroom down there. The house was empty and had a cool draft when we opened the doors.

After we explored each room we ran upstairs to see the rest of the house. Once we reached the top of the stairs, there was a living room to the right. The kitchen was located on the other side of the living room, and so was the dining room. When we turned to the left, there were two bedrooms and a bathroom. We had plenty of space for the five of us.

Clay and Annie stood around talking to Nate. Clay was a firm believer that children were to be seen and not heard, so we ran off to play in another room. When they were done talking Annie called us to get back in the car. We wondered what the adults were discussing, but we knew better than to ask about grown folk's business in front of Clay.

We had to wait until we got back to the house before we could ask Annie about the house. She would tell us things when we weren't in Clay's presence.

Clay had a taste for the finer things in life. When we were with him, we enjoyed nice homes, expensive dinners like steak and lobster and great adventures. The worst part about the two of them being together was the fighting.

We moved into the townhouse a few weeks later. As an end of the summer treat, we got to take a trip to Valley Fair. It was an amusement park located a few miles from our home.

Clay took us to the department store and bought us new outfits before we went to the amusement park. I loved days like these! Annie didn't usually go with us. We enjoyed the day just running and being free.

Burnsville, MN 1982-1984

As the weekend came to a close Annie told us that we would be starting school on Monday. Annie drove us to school the first day so that she could enroll us. The elementary school was a few blocks down the street. I was in the first grade and Jasmine in kindergarten. Our lives seemed to be settling down.

On Saturdays, we would attend our Brownie meetings. The Brownies were a younger, subgroup of the Girl Scouts. We loved being a part of a group. We didn't attend many meetings because Annie had Iman at home. Her stomach was starting to get bigger again, so I knew she was pregnant.

Annie was a stay at home mother. Over the next few months, her stomach grew in size. Clay and Annie took us out to do various things on the weekends when he was off work. Clay and Annie took us to the little neighborhood carnival. One of the best things about the carnival was being able to ride the go carts and eating cotton candy until your teeth hurt.

Clay had been working two jobs, for months, so they didn't have much time to fight. They seem to be getting along better since we had moved into our own place.

The stress of working two jobs had begun to wear on Clay. He enjoyed the finer things in life and I admired him for that.

One morning as we were getting ready for school, Annie told us that she would be in the hospital when we got home. She said that she was in labor and she was going to have the baby today. I said ok and hurried out the door to school.

The days seemed to go so quickly when you are a child. It seemed like we had just found out that she was pregnant. I think that Annie just didn't tell us when she was pregnant right away.

When we got home from school, Annie was surely in the hospital as she stated. She gave birth to a beautiful baby girl name Zaire. She was an adorable little girl. I was excited to have another sibling. Zaire was born in February of 1984. She was two years younger than our brother.

Annie didn't stay in the hospital for very long. She brought Zaire home about two days after she had her. We resumed our lives as usual. Jasmine and I played outside after school so that Annie could get some rest.

As the winter months approached, the décor of the home changed. Annie had begun to decorate the house for Christmas. Annie loved being a stay at home mother. She got into the holiday spirit as Christmas approached. Annie loved to bake; she would make chocolate chip cookies from scratch. When it was time to pick the tree, we went out as a family to collect a freshly cut Christmas tree. The holidays always brought a warm and fuzzy, sense of joy to the house. Clay and Annie were both in great spirits. On Christmas morning we woke up early, just as most children, with excitement to open our presents.

The holidays came and went quickly. The joy began to fade as the bills began to trickle in.

I don't know what happened, but one day Clay didn't come home. I hadn't heard any fighting, and I hadn't seen him. A week went past, and I asked Annie where Clay was. She said that he simply moved out. I didn't know how to feel or what to expect. We hadn't experienced a separation before.

In light of the separation, Annie decided that she was going to go back to school. She enrolled in a college degree program to pass the time. Annie never specified her major, she simply stated that it was time for her to obtain a degree. She was a stay at home mom for a number of years, so she had no skills to enter the workforce. The separation only lasted a few months before Clay and Annie found their selves back together. Her school enrollment only lasted a short time before she withdrew from the program.

With Clay gone, the bills had fallen behind, and they were unable to catch up. They made the decision to move. Our time had come to an end in the townhouse. Clay and Annie packed the moving truck and moved us to a duplex in South Minneapolis. We moved from the suburbs in Burnsville to the inner city of South Minneapolis.

Zaire was about six to eight months old at this time.

A year later, Clay and Annie went to a party at one of their friend's house. Clay came home early, but Annie chose to stay at the party. I poked my head out the door to see who was home. I asked Clay where Annie was. He said that she had stayed at the party. I wondered why they left together but returned separately. I went back to bed and waited for her to get home. Clay sat at the kitchen table, next to the back door, waiting for Annie to return also.

Annie stumbled in the door tipsy. Clay jumped up from the table and began asking questions. You could hear every word of their conversation. When the yelling began, I went to see what all the commotion was about.

Clay had Annie's hand on the counter, her fingers were spread out, and he had his hand on her wrist. He had a knife in the other hand, and the edge lay across her fingers. He threatened to cut her fingers off if she didn't answer his question. She had tears streaming down her face. You could see the fear in her eyes. She tried to explain that nothing happened at the party. She just wanted to stay and have fun.

I yelled at him to let my mother go! This was one of many nights I had been awakened by the sounds of screams and pounding flesh. He released her arm and let her go. He yelled for me to go back to bed. I was normally terrified of this man, but when it came to matters of my mother, my fear turned into courage. I was the oldest child, and I couldn't just stand by and listen as he beat her.

I had witnessed 99% of the fights. I had sat with Annie while she was bleeding and crying, and waited for the police to arrive. The response time for domestic violence calls was much longer than average. At least it sure felt that way. It seemed as if it took hours for Law Enforcement to come. The paramedics arrived on site about the same time as law enforcement. The paramedics provided basics medical treatment for her abrasions and lacerations while Law Enforcement took her statement. When they arrived, he was always long gone.

She got up the next morning in excruciating pain. She headed to the bathroom, and I followed behind her to make sure that she was okay. She closed the door as she entered the bathroom. I stood outside the door to make sure that she was alright. A few moments after closing the door, she yelled my name; I could hear the panic in her voice.

I burst into the bathroom! Upon entering, I noticed that she was holding something in between her legs. I was nervous so I approached her slowly. Once I got closer I noticed that it was a ball of thick funny looking stuff. The ball was thick and clear on the outside and something solid in the middle. I asked, "What is that?" She said, "Get me a Ziploc bag from the kitchen." I was confused, but I left the bathroom to grab the Ziploc bag as requested.

When I returned, she placed the ball of goo in the Ziploc bag. She said, "I lost the baby." My eyes filled up with tears as she placed the fetus in the bag. I asked her what she was going to do with it.

All the stress from fighting had led to this. Annie sat on the toilet holding the remnants of her unborn fetus in her hand. Annie had endured domestic abuse for a total of 10 years. She had broken jaws, black eyes, cuts, and scrapes, but nothing compared to the psychological warfare that she experienced.

Through the years they had some good times and some extremely bad times. Life went on after each fight. They did all kinds of things to make money. Sometimes they worked and other times they hustled.

Annie was in Marshall Field's shoplifting one afternoon. She had all four of us with her. Iman was about three years old, at this time. He wasn't paying any attention as he got on the escalator. He fell forward, and his fingers went into the grooves of the stairs.

We looked around to see if anyone had heard our cries. We stood panic-stricken because we didn't have a clue as to how we could help. Jasmine and I wanted to pull his fingers out of the escalator, but we didn't know if that was safe.

We stood there in a panic as the escalator continued to go up.

The security guards arrived and pressed the emergency stop button. Annie kept calling for help because Iman's hand was still stuck in between the metal grates. People were standing around trying to see what had happened.

As the medical responders arrived, they asked that we move off the escalators. The Emergency Medical Responders assessed the situation and began working on a plan to free Iman's fingers from the grates. We didn't want to move away from them. We wanted to make sure that he was alright.

The EMR's needed room to safely remove Iman's hand out of the grates. They gently removed his hand from the grate, but all we could see was blood. Jasmine and I began to cry hysterically as the EMR's carried him to the stretcher with his hand wrapped in gauze.

Annie and Iman rode in the back of the ambulance to the hospital. We rode in the back of the police car to the hospital. The police officer was nice enough to bring us into the hospital and seat us in the lobby. The officer went to find Annie. They had come in through the Emergency entrance, so he had to find out what bay they entered into. A few minutes later, Annie came from the back to let us know that Iman was going to be alright.

I asked her if he lost his fingers. She said that he was getting stitches, but all his fingers were still intact. This was a traumatic event. When I think about how brave my little brother was, it makes me proud. He was fearless. He wasn't scared, and he didn't cry for a second.

A few months later, Annie got a $10,000 settlement from Marshall Field's. They had settled her claim out of court. I thought that we were rich.

As Annie was telling us about their settlement she and Clay were packing their bags. I asked her where they were going. She said that they were going to spend the weekend at the Embassy Suites. I knew that we were rich now. The Embassy Suites was the classiest hotel that I had ever seen. We had passed it as we rode the bus through downtown Minneapolis.

Clay and Annie had made arrangements for Uncle Timmy to watch us for the weekend. We were disappointed that we couldn't participate in the wealth.

They must have had a great weekend because when they came back, they didn't have any money. Annie said that they had spent all their money on the trip. They did have a brand new Cadillac though.

It wouldn't be long before it was business as usual. A few weeks went by, and the fighting started again.

This fight ended a little different than all the ones before. The fight started with Clay pounding Annie in the face, but it turned quickly. After one or two hard jabs to the cheek, she began to fight back.

Annie had had enough; she stood up and began fighting back. She noticed the disbelief, in Clay's eyes, turn to pure anger. Something must have come over Annie that night because the scenario changed. She fled up the stairs to their room. I could hear the rumblings overhead. They had a large loft area upstairs. The rumbling started in their bedroom then moved to the top of the stairs. Clay emerged from the room with tears in his eyes.

He had a red substance running down his face. I looked at Annie as she stood with a broken bottle of hot sauce in her hand. In the midst of the fight, she had grabbed the hot sauce bottle and hit him over the head with it. That was enough to send him screaming.

He packed a large black duffle bag and threw it over his shoulder. I watched as he exited the apartment and down the front stairs. When he left out the front door, I continued to watch as he walked down the street. That was one of the proudest moments of my life. She had finally stood up for herself! She had endured his abuse for 10 years. At this age, I had no clue what the term domestic violence meant. I was just happy that Annie had fought back. I was happy that she ended the cycle of this abusive relationship.

My biggest fear was that he would kill her. I don't condone domestic violence; I was truly glad that she was alive. As a child, it's hard to witness your mother being assaulted time and time again as you stand by helpless.

There's nothing that you can do but pray that she makes it out alive. I can't give you a detailed account of every fight because it's truly not my story to tell. What I can tell you is this: these incidents left a permanent memory. Waking up to screams and the sounds of pounding flesh was traumatic. It's something that you will always remember.

Annie found out she was pregnant again. This would make their third child together. They had a vicious cycle of abuse followed by passionate romance. She always required Clay's financial assistance in raising the children.

Clay was the bread winner in the relationship. When he left, so did the finances. Annie couldn't afford the household expenses, so we found ourselves homeless. We packed what we could from the apartment. We could only carry a bag for each of us. We lived in Minnesota, it was winter, in the middle of January. We were traveling by bus with our bags on our back. We had moved away from her family years ago, and she had no other support.

We checked into a homeless shelter in downtown Minneapolis. The building was encased in brick on the outside. When you entered the lobby, it looked as if, it should be condemned. The shelter was a former hotel that was converted into a homeless shelter. The Drank Hotel was run off of county funds, but none seemed to reach the living quarters. When you entered the room, the first thing that jumped out was the bed. I should say mattress because the beds lacked bedding. They looked as if they had been stripped, but no one had come to replace the linen. The shelter provided the room, but no bedding. These conditions were unsuitable for a pregnant woman and her children.

The carpet, in the rooms, looked as if it had been there for an unprecedented amount of time. It was hard to make out the original color. Our first day at the shelter led to an immediate visit to the emergency room. Annie laid, Zaire, my baby sister on the bed and she instantly broke out. She immediately developed several abnormal spots on her arms and legs. My mother said that they were called welts. The welts, red and raised, appeared all over her body. Annie grabbed Zaire off the bed and began redressing her. She looked over at us and said get your coats back on. We asked her where we were going. Annie said that we had to get Zaire to the hospital for Emergency Treatment. I began asking myself questions. What was wrong with the bed? Why would it cause Zaire to break out so badly? When we arrived at the Emergency Room, they took Zaire to the room quickly. Annie said that she had, had an allergic reaction from something on the bed. The doctor prescribed her some Benadryl and released us. I asked Annie if we needed to take some as well. She said no because we hadn't broken out. After leaving the ER we headed back to the shelter. Nonetheless, we returned to the shelter, where we'd reside until finding a home.

A pregnant Annie had met Ben while we were in the shelter. He didn't seem to mind that she was pregnant. He showed true interest in her. The adults would play cards in the basement while the children played in the rooms. The hotel had gray concrete floors that ran along the common areas. The floors were concrete with a coat of gray paint over them. The color couldn't hide the massive amount of dirt that laid over the top. The elevators took you down to the basement where the adults would hang out. When it was dinner time, we all made our way to find our parents. The group of residents would line up outside for dinner. Dinner was served next door in a rundown kitchen.

After several weeks, maybe months, we moved into our own house! It was a little blue matchbox, off the main street, in the back of the alley. It had two bedrooms, a living room, dining room, kitchen, and loft area upstairs. The house was quite small. The upstairs had a bedroom and loft area. The other family that lived with us had three children. All of the children shared beds out in the loft area. There were six of us that moved into this home. Annie was always a kind hearted person, so she decided to let a family from the shelter move in with us. Why not? We had all just survived the shelter from our worst nightmare.

Annie had little Egypt shortly after moving into our house. He was born in November of 1986. Ben fell in love with him immediately. He was a gorgeous baby. He was a little smaller than her other babies.

He also had seizures from time to time. Annie said that it was nothing to be alarmed about. The doctors said that the seizures were related to fevers. They were known as febrile seizures. She said that most children grew out of it by age five. Five years seemed like a long time to be sick.

Annie would disappear quite often. She had a knack for making friends. When she was home, she would listen to music and play cards with her friends. Annie and Ben were both unemployed. She would leave us at home with him while she was gone. He became our new babysitter. Children weren't allowed to ask questions about their parent's business. When she was gone, she was gone. All the adults left their children in Ben's care.

The children played upstairs, and Ben typically listened to music downstairs. The door at the bottom of the stairs would be closed when the children were upstairs playing. There is a knock on the door. I ran down the stairs to answer the knock; the other children continued to play. "Who is it?" I asked. It was Ben; he wanted to check on us to make sure that we were okay. As I turned to head up the stairs, he grabbed me by the arm and pulled me in for a kiss. He pressed his big, wet lips against my mouth. My skin crawled as his lips touched mine. I was thrown off guard because he was a 26-year old man and I was an 11-year old girl. I wiped my mouth and ran up the stairs. I was so confused. I'd had a crush on a boy at school, but never anything like this. I sat on the bed replaying the scene in my mind. What should I do? Was it something I said or did? Was this innocent? Did he mean to do that? What did he mean by that? My head was filled with all these questions. What had just happened? I was afraid to go back downstairs. I decided to be careful to never to allow that to happen again.

For an 11-year old to be "careful" about her actions so that she does not provoke a grown man, is an understatement. When I say be careful, I meant not to allow myself to be trapped in a room with this man. Who was this man? Did Annie really know who he was? I was going to stick with the other children and not be singled out. There was nothing that my actions could have changed. I was merely just being a child. I stayed in my room for the next two days. I went downstairs for meals only and then promptly returned upstairs. A day or so went past, and nothing further happened. I thought to myself, I overreacted, the coast is clear. He really didn't mean anything by it. I let my guard down and went downstairs to hang with everyone else. Everyone was sitting around listening to music, laughing and singing. Conveniently, when the other adults were away, Ben would attempt to charm me as if I were a woman his age. He would sing love songs as a display of his affection to me. He showed me the type of affection that he and Annie should have shared. I believe this was his attempt to make me feel comfortable with the situation. I blushed and looked away because I felt uncomfortable. Why would he be telling me that he loved me? I looked around, and all the other children had gone upstairs. It was just the two of us sitting there listening to love songs. He reached over and grabbed me, pulling me closer to him. He slowly danced me into the other room.

The living room sat cool, dark, and empty. It had a couch and loveseat in it, but no one sat in there. Ben pushed me to the floor and pressed his body against mine. As I struggled to get up, he used force from his upper body to hold me down. He was taking my pants off with his hands. He laid on top of me and began whispering things in my ears. He told me to be quiet and not to scream. He unzipped his pants and pulled out his penis. I squirmed trying to get away, but he was much stronger than me. He pressed his body into mine and said, "Don't move or I'll hurt you!" He tried to put his penis in my vagina, but it wouldn't fit. Tears ran down my face as he attempted to force his penis inside me. He motioned his body in a circular fashion like he was making passionate love to a woman. When he got done, I jumped up and ran upstairs. I couldn't believe what had just happened. I went into the bathroom and stayed for as long as I could. We had a house full of children, but no one noticed. He had told them to stay upstairs, or he'd whoop them. No one would believe me over him. He was an adult, and I was a child. Children don't accuse adults of these kinds of things. That was the most excruciating pain I had ever experienced. All I could think was, "Where is my mother?" This would be the best time for her to walk in the house. Of course, she never did! I still to this day cannot begin to tell you where she was. It wasn't until I was 16-years old that I had the courage to tell her. I didn't tell her out of desire, but rage.

I couldn't find the courage to tell Annie; I was far too ashamed of what had happened. I tried to resume a normal life. I played outside like all the other kids. I would go on long walks and only come home when I needed to. I made a friend in the neighborhood. Jasmine had a friend with a huge house and plenty of food; she played at her house all day. I didn't like her friend, so I wasn't allowed to come in. I did make a friend about a block from our house. She stopped me while I was walking down the street and struck up a conversation. She was an only child; she was looking for someone to play with. Her mother worked during the day, so I hung out there when she wanted company. If I couldn't hang out with her, I'd stir up trouble with Jasmine so she'd have to come outside.

Jasmine was my younger sister, but she was bigger in stature. I always called her my big little sister. She was a momma's girl, soft spoken and sweet natured. She was mild mannered and easy to get along with. Her caring personality over-rode my rebellious spirit. I always felt rejected when she'd want to spend time with her friends and shut me out. I didn't get along with her friends so that made for a long and boring summer. Jasmine didn't hesitate to come get me when the neighborhood bully pushed her around.

Shannon was the oldest sister of four girls. They lived on the opposite end of the street. All the boys in the neighborhood thought that Shannon and her sisters were extremely beautiful. They appeared to be more fortunate than us. They lived in a nice home with both of their parents. Shannon was a year or two older than us, but her sisters were our age. They stirred up problems, then ran into the house to get Shannon to fight their battles.

Jasmine and Mia, Shannon's younger sister, fought from time to time. Jasmine beat up Mia, then Mia went and got Shannon. Shannon came out to fight Jasmine, so Jasmine came to get me. When I approached Shannon and asked her why she smacked Jasmine, she turned and smacked me. The burn of her heavy hand was worth the honor of a big sister. I knew that I couldn't win every battle, but it didn't mean I wasn't going to try.

That was my responsibility as an older sibling. My mother always said that if someone hit us, we'd better hit them back. We were never allowed to let one of us get hurt, and the other one do nothing. We argued and fought like any other siblings, but when it came time to protecting one another, we were always right there.

Playing outside was overrated at times. Iman, my brother, rode his bike up and down the alley. The boys made ramps and played on them for hours. I found things to do to occupy my time. We were adventurers; we'd walk for blocks to entertain ourselves.

Annie was busy planning her next adventure. Her, Ben and some of her friends decided that it would be a great adventure to drive across country. They were tired of living in Minnesota and wanted a change of scenery. She told us that we were going on this great adventure and that it would be the time of our lives. She bought a car and packed all of our clothes in the trunk. She must have been imitating her friend because she had all our clothes stacked neatly in piles. Their trunk resembled a dresser drawer. We met up at Annie's uncle's house to let him know that we were leaving. He had recently moved to Minnesota; now she was headed on this journey. We traveled from Minnesota to California on a five-day road trip. We took our time so that we could enjoy the scenery. I don't know what Annie's plan was once we arrived in California. We were children; we just went with the flow. I always hoped the situation would be better than the last.

Annie and her friends separated the moment we crossed the state line. They went on their way, and we went on ours. Our adventure ended abruptly on the side of the road. We looked around wondering if this was it or were we just resting until it was time to leave again. Some nights, we slept in our car, on the side of the highway. We would all stretch out in the back. It was so scary because the semi-trucks would pass at high speeds, shaking the car. Some nights we had the luxury of sleeping in a rundown hotel that the county provided vouchers for. All of these places had an expiration date. If the county put you up in a hotel, it was a means of temporary housing until you could find something permanent. The cost of living in California was much higher than Minnesota. By day, we'd play at the park and by night, sleep where we could find shelter. Annie always had a plan to get us out of the situation. She thought lying and manipulating her way through life, would suffice.

Annie had developed a serious drug habit when she was with Clay. As children, we knew that something was wrong, but we couldn't tell you what. Growing up with a parent(s) on drugs can impact the very state of your being. The emptiness a child feels without a home cannot be put into words. The basic essentials are important for psychological & physiological development. A home brings a sense of belonging, a piece of mind. It creates stability within a family structure. This was something that we lacked.

As we dealt with the uncertainty of hunger and shelter during the day, I dealt with chronic abuse at night. There were periods when the abuse couldn't occur, and I was thankful for that. Annie and Ben were still together. She would take us to collect cans from the neighboring dumpster during the day. Collecting cans provided us with enough money for one meal. Annie would go to the grocery store and buy this pre-made fajita mix from the deli, some fajita tortillas and a bag of O'Boise sour cream potato chips. She'd prepare the food on a hot plate, at the park, where she had set up shop. The park had outlets, so we made ourselves comfortable. Annie had met another family from Hawaii. They had moved to California to start a new life, but they ended up homeless as well. One day, we got lucky; they had decided to move back to Hawaii. They were living out of their large, pea green, conversion van. They decided to gift the van to Annie because her car had broken down. She only paid $125 dollars for the car. We were thankful it had lasted as long as it did. This new van was like a dream come true; we felt as though we had hit the lottery! The van was large enough for seven people to sleep in.

We had some great adventures in this van. Annie taught me how to drive in the van. She was quite irresponsible, so she really let me drive while she was sleeping. Now that we had the van, collecting cans became a lot easier. We approached a large green dumpster in the back of a building. I jumped in looking for cans. I found a box of Salisbury steaks packaged in a white box. Annie yelled for me to pass the box to her. The steaks had expired, but they were unopened. We had found dinner! To this day, you cannot pay me to eat a Salisbury steak. As hungry as we were, I was in awe, that this woman would feed us this food from the garbage. Were there no boundaries she wouldn't cross? She had crossed the line with this decision.

Annie didn't speak much about our situation; we followed behind her as most children do with their parents. I don't know what happened to the van, all I can remember is walking up and down, hill after hill until finally a turn. California is full of hills and valleys, so I don't know how far we walked. We got to the last street, turned right and headed down Elm Street. We approached a white house, it appeared empty, with a large porch. Who lives here? I thought. The house was small; it had one bedroom, kitchen, living room and a pool.

In the bedroom, there was a mattress top for all six of us to sleep on. Annie & Ben didn't sleep most of the time because they were up getting high. When they did sleep, we had to make room in the bed or move to the floor. There was a space heater plugged in the room to keep us warm. There was a pool in the back yard. It was half filled with green water, a tire, and other miscellaneous pieces of trash. We had no furniture or food, but we had a roof over our heads. We were typically sent outside to play, so we learned to explore each neighbor. We were curious kids and easily entertained. We found an old abandoned factory around the corner from our house. It had an old, rusted-out, abandoned car in the parking lot. We could use our imagination to play for hours. It beat the alternative of sitting around the house looking at the empty walls.

This house was another haven for bad things to happen. It was dark outside, and the house was pitch black inside. The only thing that shined was the red beams from the heater. As everyone slept, Ben would force himself upon me.

He would cover my mouth and take me into the bathroom. The repeated assaults caused me to bleed. I didn't know if the bleeding was normal or due to the trauma. When Annie returned the following morning, I told her I was bleeding. I imagined that she would ask, "Why? What happened?" But she didn't. Instead, she gave me products as if I had started my period for the first time. I kept quiet and cleaned up the mess. Afterward, I examined my private area in the mirror. I wanted to see how much damage he had done. It wasn't so much of what you could see on the outside, but the damage inside.

As we played outside the following morning, a dingy, stray, white dog approached us. The dog looked like he hadn't been bathed in a long time. He was homeless and in need of shelter just like us. We skipped home to ask if we could keep it. We brought the dog into the house and asked Ben if we could keep it.

Annie didn't care for dogs, so she said, "NO!" but Ben made a plea for us to keep it. Annie had found this pearly white carpet; they had placed it in the living room. We had nothing else in the house but this nice piece of carpet and a mattress top in the bedroom. Ben said that we could keep the dog. We brought the stray dog in and made it at home. The next morning when we woke, we discovered a large, perfectly formed circle of dog poop on the carpet in the living room. The circle of poop wasn't the typical pile, but a large circle, as if, he had drug his butt, dropping turd after turd. We all stood there looking at the poop in shock. We stood there and watched as Ben beat the dog. We felt sorry as we listened to it yelp and scream. Why would the dog poop on the only thing that we had in the house? Wasn't the stray dog house trained? After Ben finished punishing the dog, he opened the door and put him out. The dog ran away yelping in pain.

The end of summer came, and fall neared; it was time to return to school. Enrolling in a new school was nerve wracking. The oddness of being in a strange place, new school, and new people. We had to go to school and pretend that everything was normal at home. All the dysfunction at home and you couldn't tell anyone. The saving grace was that Annie had a drug habit; she couldn't pay the rent at any place we'd ever lived. So that meant that if we didn't like the school or even if we did, we wouldn't be there long.

We didn't maintain any residence for any length of time. Each day was different, and we had no expectations for what was to come. We didn't know what day she'd wake up and tell us that we were moving again. We had gone through the process of enrollment only to be evicted from this residence as well. Apparently, Ben and Annie had gotten into a huge fight, and he left. The great news was, Ben was gone, and we were returning to Minnesota. I could finally sleep at night.

We returned to Minnesota, and things had made a change. By change, I really mean they varied but remained the same.

Chapter 3 -
My 13-Year Old Self

Annie found a three-bedroom duplex on DuPont Avenue on the north side. Ben returned as soon as he got word that she had another place. I began running away quite frequently; I couldn't take living in the same house as him. I had friends all over the city. Their mothers would let me spend a few nights at a time. We didn't go to school most of the time anyway. We made an appearance a few times a month. My friends and I would spend the day at each other's house. It wouldn't be long before Annie would lose custody of the younger children.

Annie had lost custody of all five of her children. My younger siblings had family that lived in Minnesota. They would spend time with them periodically. My younger brother Iman had told his family that he hid razor blades in the ceiling so that Annie could not use drugs. After revealing this news, Iman, Zaire, and Egypt never came back home. Weeks went past, and I finally asked Annie, "Where are the kids?" She was good at keeping secrets. She sat in her chair with a pile of dope by her side getting high. We didn't know what was going on most of the time. Annie replied, "The kids aren't coming back."

I asked, "WHY?" She proceeded to explain what had happened. After my brother had told his family what was going on in our home, they refused to let them return to this type of environment. They showed up about a week later to get extra clothing for them. If you have children living in an unsafe environment why would you attempt to gather their clothes? All of our clothes came from the free store. We would go to the free clothing and food giveaways to shop; we were tasked with picking out our own clothes. There was a neighborhood charity center that served meals and assisted with clothing. We were regular visitors at this center.

After this incident, the young ones were placed in foster care. After being in the system, they were eventually taken into custody by some of their relatives. Iman, Zaire, and Egypt went to live with their aunt and grandmother. We thought that we were safe because they hadn't come for us yet, but we were taken away shortly thereafter. We had gone through several foster homes before landing in a facility. People would take us in for the money, but lock us in a room for the day. There was little to no interaction with the people responsible for caring for us. Needless to say, we just wanted to know when we'd be able to return home. We felt that our younger siblings were pretty fortunate because they had a family that loved them. People that claimed them and wanted to see them safe. Jasmine and I had no one that would show up to make sure we were okay. Why didn't anyone want to see us safe? Why weren't we loved in the same type of manner?

There's nothing like being in a facility or place, uncertain of your future. We had no means of communication with Annie. We were abandoned to the care of strangers. As we were being processed through "intake" we were scared and full of questions. People have a tendency to feel that children do not have the ability to process information.

The foster homes didn't work out, so we were sent to live in a children's facility. The facility was large; it was sectioned off by age; we were two to a room. I always wanted to be close to Jasmine because we were all that we had. The facility had all kinds of activities to keep us busy. We had pottery classes, ceramics, gym and any children's movie you could think of. I participated in the activities for a while, but after a few months grew tired of them. I had begun to make friends in the older children's module. The older children would run away at night and then return when it got too late. We would walk to the lake and hang out there for hours. We just wanted to get away from being locked away.

The sad part was that most of us hadn't really done anything to get here. Some were troubled teens, but others had the misfortune of coming from a dysfunctional family, and this was the only place that would take them in. I met one of my lifelong friends at this facility. Candy was 12-years old, and she had a baby. She had every intention of returning home to her baby. She didn't plan on staying. We had been there for several months; I had begun to lose track of time. Candy talked to her boyfriend on the phone day and night. She was in love with an older guy. She voluntarily introduced me to her brother Jeremy. She arranged a few phone conversations between the two of us. I really wasn't interested in him because I had a crush on one of the older boys in Mode C. After a few conversations with Jeremy, we decided to meet. He sounds like a cool guy over the phone.

I packed an overnight bag for our trip. When I left the children's facility, I didn't plan on coming back. Candy had a home to return to, but I didn't. She assured me that it would be fine, "You can stay at my house," Candy said. She introduced me to her brother, Jeremy. He was a large, heavy-set guy that loved to have fun. I was quiet and reserved, and he was outgoing. He had done time in a locked juvenile facility; he was a juvenile delinquent also. The first night we kicked it and hung out all night talking and listening to music. At the end of the night, Jeremy and I crashed on the floor in Candy's boyfriend's room. In the morning I realized I couldn't stay there, so I had to go back to Annie's house.

She was still in the same house. Everyone lived in the same proximity, so it wasn't too far to walk. I knocked on the door, and Annie was surprised to see me. When she opened the door, I asked her why she hadn't tried to find us. She walked away with her head down. She was in the next room getting high, and she wasn't expecting me to show up. She fed me a lie about what she was doing to get all of us back. How could you be trying to get your kids back if you're in the room getting high? Part of her court-ordered stipulations was mandatory drug testing. She couldn't pass a drug test if she continued getting high.

I walked past her and headed to my room. We still had the two twin mattresses on the floor. The rest of the house was empty. The house felt so cold and empty without my siblings. I remembered hearing their laughter as they played in the house. I laid on the bed and thought about Jasmine. I had left her at the children's home alone. How could I talk to her without a phone? I wasn't going back now that I realized Annie was still in the same place. All of the clothes had come from the free store so I could replace them. I realized that I'd figure something out after I woke up from my nap. I was exhausted from kicking it all night.

When I woke up, I talked to Annie about getting a phone line. We had to be able to talk to the other kids. She said that she'd work on it. I jumped in the shower so I could head to Candy's house. Jeremy and I had a good time, so I wanted to see him again. We knew so many people around the neighborhood we could hang out anywhere. Candy lived about three miles away from me. We walked everywhere we went. It was summer time, so we had nothing but daylight. I walked over to Candy's house to see what she was doing. Her mother greeted me and invited me in. Candy was upstairs with the baby so she said that I could go up. Candy was in the baby's room ironing letters on the back of her cotton jogging suit. She had her and her boyfriend's initials on everything.

I asked her what the plans for the day were. She said that we were going to get a sandwich and head over to see the fellows. It sounded like a great plan to me. She finished ironing her jogging suit as I stood and watched. She slipped it on when she was done, and we headed out. Candy had to stop and talk to her mom before she left out. She gave her money and told her not to be gone all night. We walked through the projects speaking to people that she knew. I didn't really know anyone besides her on this side of town. She lived across the highway in the cleaner, safer side, but we had to pass through the projects to get back to the inner part of town.

We hit the block where Jeremy and his friends were. When we walked up, there were two girls walking away. They walked past and didn't really say anything. I walked up and asked Jeremy what was up. They were sitting in the front yard playing music and drinking 40 ounces. We came over and sat down on the front stairs. Candy and her boyfriend disappeared into the house. Jeremy and I sat on the stairs and talked for a while.

Our relationship wasn't very exciting. We had dated for a short time before the relationship exploded. Jeremy was seeing another fast-tail girl named Deedee, in the neighborhood. She was under the impression that he was her man and I had no idea who she was. She and his cousin were friends, so she told her everything about me. The two of them decided that we all needed to confront him. They knew how things worked better than I did. Some nights he would be with her and others with me.

They staged an outing at one of our friendly hang out places. We would hang out in front of Taco Bell some nights. One person would buy a soda and then we'd get free refills all night. Everyone showed up for the meeting as planned. I guess I was the only dummy that wasn't informed. You could see the hostility on Deedee's face as we all sat around talking. He told me he wasn't sleeping with her and told her the same about me. I knew better because she knew too much. I had no real feeling for him, so I didn't care either way. If she wanted to be with him, that was fine!

When Deedee walked up, his whole demeanor changed. He asked her what she was doing there. She said, "I wanted to see you." He tried to play it cool, but you could see the irritation on his face. He demanded that she go get him some water. She made several smart comments about me before she went inside saying, "Why don't you have your girl go get you some water?" I looked at her like, girl, please. I said, "I have nothing to do with anything y'all got going on." Her friend told her to go inside the building and get the water. She followed behind her mumbling things under her breath. I got up and headed for the bathroom. We all ended up in the bathroom. Deedee had gotten a cup from the front counter and dipped it into the toilet water that had pee in it. The bathrooms were nasty, and she chose the stall with the broken toilet. Her friend tried to convince her not to do it, but she was upset. I stood and watched as I washed my hands. She cleaned off the outside of the cup and placed the lid on it. She walked outside with the cup in her hand. She brought the cup to him and handed it to him. Her friend (his cousin) stopped him from drinking it. I wasn't going to say anything because that was a lover's quarrel.

He had done her wrong, not me, so he was getting what he deserved. Her friend explained to him that she had gotten the water out of the toilet. He turned and slapped me across the face. The impact was so hard that my face felt as if it was on fire. When Deedee saw Jeremy strike me, she took off running. He said that I should have told him what was in the cup. Why? Did you tell me that you were sleeping with her? I thought. He chased her around the parking lot for a while. I could see the anger in his eyes so while he was busy chasing her, I slipped away. I talked to him a few months later after he was locked up for felony assault. He didn't catch her that night, but he did later assault someone else.

I moved on like any teenage girl would do. Jeremy called me later to tell me that he was locked up. I didn't care, he was not the right person for me. I explained how disrespectful the whole situation was. If he was with someone else, all he had to do was tell me. He was a cool guy to hang around, but our relationship wasn't anything serious. As I was talking on the phone, Annie came in to tell me something. She and Ben were overjoyed with the news. I told Jeremy that I'd talk to him some day and hung up the phone. I looked at Annie and said, "What's up?" She had just found out that she was pregnant with Ben's first child. He was happy that he was going to be a father. I looked around the house, at all the emptiness, and said, "Congratulations." Annie was pregnant, by Ben, with child number six. She hadn't stopped getting high although she was pregnant. She stayed up all night getting high and slept during the day. Sometimes, she'd go on these binges and get high for days.

Jasmine called during our conversation which gave me the escape I needed. I took the phone into the other room to tell her the news. I tried to convince her to come home, but she was happy at the facility. She asked me why I left. They had regular meals and stable housing. She was content with the comfort and stability the facility offered. The activities were great, but I didn't want to be locked up. I wanted her to leave so that we would be home together. I knew that she was younger and actually needed to be in a safe environment, but I was selfish. We were the closest of all our siblings, and I missed her. She said that she would think about it and let me know when she called back. I was good with that answer for now. I was heading to a friend's house anyway.

Rochelle lived on the next block, and she was dating Jeremy's brother. He wasn't really his brother, but they had known each other for so long it seemed that way. The kids in the neighborhood did whatever they could to make a little money. There was a couple that would take kids to sell candy. They recited some script about raising money for some organization. They would take us to nice neighborhoods and send us door to door. I wasn't really good at selling candy. It seemed like too much work to sell a few candy bars. When we met back at the car, our sponsors would take most of the money and give us a few dollars for our time. The first time was grand. I sold all the candy bars in the box and brought them a stack of money. Some people gave donations instead of buying candy bars. The sponsors took the donations too. We were out selling candy bars from early morning to late evening. I only went once or twice. Rochelle used the money to buy food for her house or late night snacks. I liked being over her house because we would order videos all day. The same video all day for $3.99 each. I stayed over at her house for days at a time. Her mom didn't mind because she would be out getting high too.

When I returned home, Jasmine had come back. I was excited to have her home. We fell asleep talking about all the things that had happened since we had last seen each other. Meanwhile, Annie was up getting high in the kitchen. She was on one of her binges, and this one sent her into labor. I don't think that she had reached full term before she went into labor.

Ben woke Jasmine and me to go to the hospital with Annie. Annie's eyes were as big as quarters when she walked out of the kitchen. We asked why she needed to go to the hospital. He said that she was in labor and needed to be seen. We got up and got dressed. They allowed Jasmine to ride in the back of the ambulance and I rode in the front. She must have been in labor for some time because once we got to the hospital, the doctors were preparing her for delivery. The nurse checked her cervix and said she was fully dilated.

Ben had Annie, but he would always be a pedophile. He would creep into my room and have sex with me after having had sex with her. I distinctly remember the smell of tuna on his breath. I didn't know what that smell represented. He would slide into my bed, and I would attempt to play sleep. I always prayed that he'd just go away, but it didn't work. It never stopped him from having sex with me.

The nurses asked us to step out of the room so they could get her situated. Jasmine and I walked to the coffee machine to get some hot chocolate. By the time we got back to the room, she had her legs up in the stirrups pushing. She gave birth to a premature little boy. He was underweight, so they had to place him in the newborn ICU. We visited him through the glass of the incubator. We didn't know the true effects of what really was going on. We had literally just stepped out the room, and she had already given birth. Any birth that lasts under three hours is called precipitous labor. We hadn't been at the hospital longer than an hour, and she had delivered her son. No one took the time to clearly explain what was going on either. The nurses said that the baby needed a little extra warmth; Annie cooperated with their story. She wasn't going to tell us the truth.

Annie was released from the hospital a couple of days later, but her baby boy wasn't. We overheard the nurses saying that she had drugs in her system. We knew that she got high, but how did that affect the baby? They took my baby brother Desmond into custody, and he never came home.

Chapter 4 - These Were Very Interesting Years - 1989-1990

After Ben and Annie had lost custody of their baby, Ben left again. They fought over his son, her drug use, and her lack of parental guidance. I couldn't say I blamed him, but hell, who was he to judge her? He was the monster that lived in the little girl's closet. Annie coated her pain with drugs and blocked everything else out. I didn't know if this was the way she had coped with all her pain or if she was trapped in her own cycle of life.

She turned DuPont Avenue into "The Dope House." She met this guy from California that sold drugs. They called him Cali because he was from California. One day we came home, and he was just sitting in the kitchen. Cali had on an all-black hoodie and black dickies. Cali came and brought a few of his boys. They took in upwards of about $10,000 a week. It started off as one guy, then it grew until there were about 10. They'd be in the kitchen shooting dice and listening to music. We'd stick our heads in to see what all the noise was about. The floor usually had a pile of fifty and hundred dollar bills on it. All that money and we were stuck in the room starving. How was it that they were making all this money, but couldn't feed the two children stuck in the house? They took turns taking their post at our house. They had a police scanner in the kitchen, by the back door so they could hear the police activity.

Annie had met another guy named Get Down, by this time. She let him stay at the house from time to time. Annie would sit in the bedroom with a plate of crack cocaine on a mirror. There was more than enough crack on that plate to feed her children. Why didn't she sell something on that plate to get us something to eat? Or why couldn't she ask them to pay her in cash instead of crack? I didn't completely understand her mindset. Why was life so difficult?

Get Down was another guy that got high, so Annie didn't mind him coming through. They were just friends, and he was pretty cool. He would go to the grocery store and steal food for us. He'd stuff steaks and pizzas in his pants. He looked out for us all the time. We had absolutely nothing in the refrigerator. We appreciated what he did for us. He came to the house with a used tv to sell. We asked him if he could get us something to eat. He left to go to the store and never came back. A day or two went by and we asked Annie what happened to him. He had been arrested for shoplifting.

Things were heating up around the house. All the traffic had brought attention to the house. The police were looking into all the activity. They knew that a house with this much traffic was usually affiliated with some kind of illegal activity. They sent a guy to the back door wearing a black hoodie. One of the guys went out there and sold him something. We heard the police talking about the guy they had just sent to the door. The whole crew packed up their things and left immediately! The activity slowed down after that night. The house was quiet, and no one was around. We got word that Cali's brother, Crutch, had returned to California and was shot in the head.

My best friend Jada was ecstatic to hear the news. Jada and I had met about one year prior at a block party. She was this short, thin, jazzy spit-fire. She wore a short haircut and big hoop earrings; she dressed the part with an attitude to match. She approached me angrily at the block party. "Are you Nyla?" she asked.

I responded with, "Yes! Who wants to know?" She asked if I knew her boyfriend. I followed up with, "Who is your boyfriend?"

"T.C." she responded. I explained to her that I did know him and how we met. He was someone that had been interested in me, but I was not interested in him. We then exchanged words for a few minutes. While we were exchanging words, I mentally prepared myself for a fight. She had two other girls with her, and I was at the block party alone.

Jaylen was one of Jada's close friends. Jaylen was tall, dark, thin, and sassy. She was a chic from Chicago that rocked the latest hair trends. She had short curls on the top and long hair in the back. She always stayed fly. She was a fighter by nature, so she was ready at any moment. After we discussed the situation, we left together.

We had no reason to fight. We spent the rest of the day talking and kicking it. He was not her boyfriend, and I had no interest in him. Jada and I became really close friends after this. I used to see her around school, she was typically running down the halls from the truancy officer. I always wondered where she was going. I knew all these people from school or the neighborhood.

I was puzzled at Jada's reaction to Crutch being shot, so I began to ask a few questions. I asked, "Why would you be so happy to hear about someone's death?" She began to explain what had occurred on her way home from my house one night. She was six-months pregnant, and I had asked if anyone could give her a ride home. It was late, and she only lived around the corner, but I didn't want her to walk. Crutch said that they were going her way and they would drop her off. Once they got her in the car, they took her to their apartment in Brooklyn Center. On foot, this was at least an hour walk. They told her that if she gave everyone blowjobs, she could get a ride home. She did what they asked, and they dropped her off. She never mentioned the incident until this day. I began to understand why she felt ecstatic.

I had older friends and younger ones. Annie was good at making friends also. It seemed that everyone she knew smoked drugs too. Most of her friends had children our age. When we met her friends, we met their children. I stumbled down the alley trying to make it home one night after leaving Jada's house. Tander was walking past with his homeboys. He called out trying to get my attention. I kept going because we were in an alley. He followed behind me still trying to get my attention. I stopped and talked to him for a minute once I got closer to my house.

When he walked up to my house, he said that he knew some guys that hung out here. We exchanged numbers, and I went into the house. He called the next morning to check on me. I barely remembered giving him my number. I invited him over to the house. Annie had a new set of guys dealing out of the house. I knew that with all this company, it would be okay. Tander came over with a few of his friends. I introduced him to everyone sitting around the table. The new crew was from around the neighborhood, and they were younger. Tander seemed to know most of them. Annie didn't allow boys in our room, so we sat in the living room and talked. We hung out for a few minutes, then he decided he had to go. I guess there was too much testosterone in the room.

We were always surrounded by males. This crew was from a different set and was fun to hang out with. They enjoyed playing the Nintendo and eating pizza. They were there for the same purpose, but they were far more entertaining. We hung out so much that we became family. They treated us like their sisters. They watched out for us and made sure we were taken care of. We used to play fight and wrestle all the time. They showed us how to defend ourselves.

We enjoyed when they came over. The eldest of the crew, Russ, began dating Annie. Annie was dating a younger guy that had taken Cali's place. She was about 10 years older than Russ, but she was dedicated to making him money. She didn't mind these fellows being in our room because they were like family. Annie didn't know that Russ had a family at home. Their relationship just stirred up more trouble for us. The fellows would go back and report what was going on and the women would call threatening us over the phone.

Russ was making money, so he was seeing all kinds of women. He had the main chic at home. He had a side chic and Annie. I thought he was only entertaining Annie because she made him so much money. Jasmine and I defended our mother against every accusation. We fought the side chic and the main chic when they came around. We told both of them not to bring the drama to our house. Take that mess up with Russ.

Tander called and asked if I wanted to hang out at his house or mine. He came to meet me, and we decided to go over to his friend's house. We walked to his homeboy's house down the street. When we got there, he brought me into his friend's room. He thought that I was going to give it up. No! I'd had a run of bad relationships, and I wasn't interested in having sex. I told him that if he was truly interested in me, sex wouldn't be the only thing on his mind. He said that he'd prove to me that he wanted more. His homeboy walked into the room and asked if he had hit it yet. I looked over at him and said, "No!" I got up and left out the door. He followed behind me trying to explain. I didn't need an explanation because I wasn't giving it up.

It was dark, so he walked me back home. When I reached the front door, there was an eviction notice posted on it. A whole new crew had moved in, but no one was paying the rent. Three days later we heard a knock on the door, it was the sheriff. Out of all the places we had been evicted from, never was there a sheriff. They advised us to grab whatever we could fit in a garbage bag, but the rest had to stay. I called Tander on the phone to tell him what had just happened. Tander and I discussed me moving in with him temporarily.

I thought it was so sweet that he would offer to let me stay at his home. Within a couple weeks, I began to understand who he truly was; he was like any other man that loved the thrill of the chase. He loved to hang in the streets with his friends. Tander was an immature teenage boy. He wanted me to sit in the basement all day while he hung out with his friends. A few months of us living together passed and I left. I guess when I look back, it was completely normal. Kids like to hang out with their friends. They can't be expected to be in a serious relationship at the age of 15. I didn't feel like I was only 13-years old. I felt like I had adult responsibilities. I couldn't be concerned with hanging out all the time when I had needed to maintain housing and food. He was living the average teenage life so I couldn't fault him for anything.

I'd had a pregnancy scare a month prior. I knew that I wasn't ready to be a mom. The doctor told me I wasn't pregnant, but my friend told Tander I was. He told everyone that I was pregnant. I tried to tell him otherwise, but he wouldn't listen. Penny was actually the one pregnant, but she didn't want her parents to know. I woke up the following morning with a huge pool of blood under me. He thought that I had a miscarriage, but I knew it was probably just my period. He was upset with the situation.

He talked to his mom, and she said that I probably lost the baby. What baby? I was never pregnant! I tried to explain this to him, but he insisted that I had lied to him. He made me pack my things and leave. I had a huge garbage bag of clothes that I had brought with me. He sat the bag outside and told me to find somewhere else to stay. I carried my bag down the street crying, ashamed, and embarrassed. I vowed that I would never live with another man again. I didn't even want to speak to him again.

Annie had taken up residence with another friend. She always managed to find somewhere else to stay. I called her, and she invited me to come stay with them. Cindra was a really nice lady; she was married with three children. She had a teenage daughter and two sons. She welcomed us into her home and let us stay until we could get on our feet. Her daughter, Nina, and I clicked from the beginning. She was the youngest of three, and her parents were pretty strict on her. When I moved in, I didn't help the situation.

I hadn't spoken to Tander for about three weeks, so I called him to see what he was up to. I invited him and his friend over to hang out. I invited them to the back of the house. Nina had a window in her closet with no screen. We snuck Tander and his friend in through the window. We talked about the pregnancy situation and made amends. I wasn't trying to trap him into any type of relationship. Some nights, Nina and I would sneak out to chill with the fellows. We could always find someone's, parentless house.

A few months had gone by, and I woke up extremely ill. I couldn't hold anything down, and I couldn't get out of bed. The days led to weeks, the weeks led to a month, then three months. Cindra pulled me to the side and asked if I could be pregnant. "No," I replied. I could remember having a light period a month or two ago, or so I thought. I had never considered the fact that I might be pregnant, so I made a doctor's appointment.

At the doctor's appointment, I took a pregnancy test. The doctor came in and said that I was about three months pregnant with my first child. They could only go by the information I had given them and the symptoms I explained. I was overjoyed to be having my first child. I was actually pregnant this time. I vowed that I would be everything I wanted in a parent. I told her that I would love her unconditionally. Nothing or no one could ever take this love away from me. She would never be able to leave me, and I would never leave her.

It's amazing how young teenage girls celebrate having a child out of wedlock. All my friends cheered with me. They congratulated us and wished us well. We were so happy to be bringing a beautiful baby into this world. The thought of financial, emotional, or parental support never crossed my mind. We were both first-time parents, so our conception was special. We made plans to build our family and start a future.

Tander and I decided that we would try to work things out. We spent most of our time together after receiving the pregnancy news. Tander had an older friend, Sly, that we both hung out with. They didn't have water or electricity at their house, so they didn't mind if we hung around. Sly and his girlfriend, Lisa, lived with her parents and she had two children of her own. He was from Chicago and always talked about how great it was back home.

He wanted to impress Lisa, so they planned a trip to Chicago together. They asked Tander and me to watch their baby boy Zander while they went out of town. I didn't want to be stuck with a baby, so they asked Jada to keep an eye on the baby. Zander always seemed to be crying. I wondered if something was wrong with him.

Jada agreed to keep Zander while they were out of town. The very first night, she noticed that he wouldn't stop crying. She felt that there was something wrong, so Jada took him to the hospital. Lisa's parents lived downstairs but really didn't have anything to do with what Lisa did. Jada was scared, so she took him to the Emergency Room. Zander was admitted to the hospital for pneumonia.

The doctors and nurses asked Jada all types of questions pertaining to the baby's health. We didn't know anything about the baby or the parents really. Jada was forced to leave the baby at the hospital. Sly and Lisa didn't leave a contact number so she couldn't reach them. Jada and I didn't have children, so we didn't have a clue what to do in this type of situation. When Sly returned, he came looking for Jada and me. The hospital had sent social services over to investigate the child's home. Sly couldn't find Jada, so Tander brought him over to my house. Tander knocked on the door and asked that I come outside and talk. I thought it was just a friendly visit, so I went outside laughing and giggling.

We casually walked to the end of the alley talking and joking. Once we got to the end of the alley, Sly began questioning me about what happened to Zander. I tried to explain to him that the baby was sick and Jada was just doing what she thought was best. Sly pulled out a switch and whooped me like I was one of his little children. I couldn't believe that Tander just stood there and watched. Tander was scared of Sly. He had this reputation because of his family connections. I didn't know him nor did I really care. I also didn't want anything else to do with Tander. I snatched my arm from him and ran back to the house as fast as I could. I told them that if they followed me, I was going to call the police! I packed my things and went to stay at Jada's house. I knew that Sly didn't know where she lived so I'd be safe there. I ended things with Tander after that night. Neither of them had a reason to come looking for me.

As soon as I got to Jada's house, I told her everything that happened over the last few days. She told me what happened in the hospital. She had tried to contact Lisa and Sly, but she didn't have a number. She also called Lisa's parents, but the phone was disconnected. She didn't have any pertinent information to give the social worker. She had no choice but to leave the baby at the hospital. She wasn't his legal guardian. Jada and I decided to lay low for a couple of days. We stayed at her house mostly. We didn't go anywhere or do anything because too much stuff had happened.

Jada's mom asked us to walk to the store and get some items for dinner. It had been a few days so we thought that everything could have cooled down. Tander hadn't tried to contact me, so that was a plus. Jada and I walked to the store to get the groceries her mom requested.

We grabbed a cart and started in the produce aisle. Before we could get in the store good, a young lady walked in and started yelling at me. She asked, "Are you Nyla?"

I responded, "Yes, who are you?"

She says, "I'm Trisha, Tander's girlfriend!"

"Who's' girlfriend?" I thought. My mouth had to drop to the floor. Where or when did he have a girlfriend? I had been living with him for months before I found out I was pregnant. I dated him for months before I moved into his house. I'm lost! "What?" I asked.

Trisha replied, "I moved to Kansas, but we are still together!"

OH! OK! That explains everything! I replied, "I didn't know that he had a girlfriend and his sisters never mentioned you either."

His baby sister had led this Amazon looking girl right to me. She wasn't trying to hear my statements, she wanted to fight. I had no intention of fighting her because I was pregnant. She was loud and irate in the store, causing a big commotion. The store manager walked up and told us that we needed to leave. I left the store, and she followed me. Once I got outside, I looked up, and there was a whole group of girls standing around.

I didn't want to fight, but I wasn't going to let them jump me either. She hit me once or twice, but I didn't fight back. The first thought that came to my head was me losing my baby. I immediately walked away as she continued yelling profanities at me. I was already done with him so why would I fight over him? Why wouldn't she take this issue up with her "boyfriend"! How did he have a girlfriend out of state and another one living at his mother's home? He was surely not worth the fight. I rubbed my stomach and told my baby that it was safe. Tander wasn't important enough for me to risk the most important thing in my world. How did I always manage to get myself into these situations with men? Jada and I met back at her house. When I had walked away, she went back into the store to get the things her mother had requested. I knew I had made the right decision by leaving Tander alone. He had proved to be the wrong guy at every turn.

Jasmine came looking for me at Jada's house. She had been staying with friends when Annie had disappeared again. Jasmine and I had spoken to Annie earlier that day, and she said that she was going to a friend's house. She hadn't seen this friend in a while and asked if we wanted to go with her. Pam was related to the couple we went to California with. I was exhausted with all the things that had gone wrong, so I decided to go.

Whenever Annie disappeared, we had to make our own sleeping arrangements. Jasmine and I would hang out with our friends and then ask if we could stay the night. There were many nights that we slept where we could. Some of these people had the nastiest houses you could imagine; roaches, rats, and unclean floors. We would often have to sleep on the floor because we had nowhere else to stay. We couldn't stay long because we were minors. Most of our friend's parents were on drugs or very poor.

Annie and Pam decided that they were going to have a girl's night out. They were laughing and joking while they helped one another get dressed. They traded lipsticks and packed their purses with weapons.

As they left out the door, laughing and full of life, I remember saying, "don't get into any trouble and make sure you come back and get us."

Joking as it may have seemed, I had a serious undertone. The panic at the thought of being left with strangers. Parents believe that it's safe to leave children at their friend's house because their friends say it's okay.

I didn't know who the strange man babysitting us was, but I distinctly remember Annie saying, "Don't touch my girls."

If you thought enough to say that, then why would you leave us in the care of this person? The conversation made me uneasy, so it was quite difficult to fall asleep on the floor. Annie borrowed blankets to make a pallet on the floor. The man sat in the chair and watched tv as we laid on the floor. After an hour or two, we fell asleep. I woke up to him breathing over me.

I could feel him rubbing his genitals on my butt. I moved and made a noise so I could wake the others. He was startled, so he moved away quickly. I laid there praying that he wouldn't come back. I prayed that Annie would return and we would leave. Although we had nowhere to go, anywhere is better than here. He waited for a few minutes and then returned with subtle movements of perversion. I turned and said, "Get away from me before I tell my mother." That got his attention because he left me alone.

We were awakened by Pam's hysterical crying. She was pacing the floor pointing and crying, she looked over at Jasmine and me, pointing. She had been brought home by two officers, and they were standing at the door. The officers walked over to us and asked if we would come with them.

We stood up confused and terrified. "Come with you for what? Where is my mother?" I questioned.

Pam screamed, "She didn't have to do that! We were going to get back together!"

What was she talking about? The two of them had left together, and only she returned.

We walked out of the house terrified! The event was playing out in slow motion. Our minds were caught in a trance as we headed to the police car sitting in front of the house. The event seemed so surreal as we exited. We walked to the car shaking and crying. We still hadn't heard what happened to our mother. As the officers placed us in the back of the car, one said, "Your mother is in jail." Pam had a look of disgust in her eyes when we left the house. She made us feel like we were responsible for what had transpired. All I could think was, "Would someone please tell us what's going on?"

My heart dropped as we entered a neighborhood that was all too familiar. We were taken right back to the same children's facility for booking; at least, that's what it felt like. This wasn't the first time we had been housed in this facility. The officers walked us into the intake unit. There was a large room filled with children of all ages. They had toys, books, tv, and movies for each age group. The children played in this room until the administration staff could get you processed into your specific module. It had only been about a year since we last left this place, we were familiar with the procedure. The gentle acts of kindness were only an icebreaker to transition you into the facility.

I had made up my mind; I wasn't about to spend another year here. We had already spent a year at this facility before we decided to run away. I remember all too vividly what happened in the last encounter. In order for me to stay at Jeremy's place, I had to have sex with him. I wasn't about to relive those events. I wasn't going to be locked away and written off as a lost cause either. This time, I had an unborn child to think about.

The following morning, a social worker paid us a visit. She had been our social worker for years. She updated us on the events that had transpired between Annie and Pam. She said that she had contacted our grandparents in Ohio and they had agreed to take custody of us. Wait a minute lady, you're moving too fast.

The first question was, "Where is my mother?"

She informed us that the night Annie and Pam went out, they got into an altercation with Pam's ex-boyfriend Greg. Annie knew the woman that Greg had been seeing, so she agreed to take Pam down to their house for a *"talk."* The altercation ended with the death of Greg and the incarceration of Annie. It all was starting to make sense now, but wait! Why did Annie kill Greg?

I knew Annie suffered from post-traumatic stress disorder, but how did that tie into all of this? Annie's history of physical abuse triggered a response that she wasn't even ready for. Greg and Pam argued about the woman he was with. Greg slapped Pam for showing up to his girlfriend's home. When Annie tried to break up the fight, Greg punched her in the face. Annie dug into her purse and pulled out the knife she had packed earlier. Greg charged at her again, and she stabbed him in his neck. He staggered to the porch and collapsed. He laid there clutching his neck as he hemorrhaged. Annie had stabbed him in his carotid artery, within two minutes he had lost a massive amount of blood. His body laid there on the porch, lifeless. Pam ran to him and began shaking him.

Greg's girlfriend watched the altercation from the porch door, she never entered the altercation. She stood in the screen door calling the police for assistance.

Pam began screaming, "We were going to get back together!"

She immediately charged at Annie, yelling, "Why did you do that?"

By the time the police responded to the domestic call, it was too late. When they arrived on the scene, Greg was dead, and Annie stood on the sidewalk holding the knife. Annie told the officers that she was only protecting her friend. The police placed Annie in the back of the car. Another officer collected statements from all of the bystanders. They didn't need to talk to very many eye witnesses because Annie was going to prison! Pam was going to make sure of that.

We listened to the details of the story and sobbed uncontrollably. I'd had a bad feeling that something was going to happen that night. I was young, but I knew trouble when I saw it. After receiving the information that we would be relocating to Ohio in a few days, I ran away from the children's facility. I wanted to say goodbye to Jada and Tander. I felt he at least deserved to know that much. The social worker got word that I left, so she called the only place she thought I could be. She threatened to send the police to pick me up if I didn't return to the shelter. I assured her that I'd be at the airport in the morning prior to departure. I hadn't spoken to Tander since the last two incidents, so I called him to let him know that we'd be moving away.

Chapter 5 -
Fourteen and Pregnant

I arrived in Ohio five months pregnant; I felt empty and alone again. I had left everything and everyone I knew behind. All my friends and the comfort of a city I had grown up in. So here we were in a city, just the two of us. My grandparents loved us to no end, but they had no idea what type of responsibility they had just taken on. My father and uncles were no angels, but my aunts had been a little easier to raise. I didn't know any of this then, but I later found out.

My past was a continuum of instability and uncertainty. I was a 14-year old young girl that had been living on the streets for the last year. I had slept on garage floors, on park benches, and anywhere else someone would let me lay my head. Ben had lived with us until I was 13-years old. It had gotten to the point that I began fighting him. Annie didn't listen to my side of the story, only his.

When Ben began making gestures at my little sister, the fights between us grew increasingly worse. I couldn't allow her to go through what I had been through. Jasmine was always my younger, sweeter, naïve sister. I refused to let her go through the horrendous things that he'd done to me. Ben played with Jasmine innocently. She didn't see the danger in it, but I remembered all too well how it started with me. We were sitting on the couch when I first noticed his actions. The hate and rage that I had toward him bubbled over immediately. I jumped off the couch and told him to take his hands off of Jasmine. He pushed me back onto the couch and said shut up! We started arguing, and I took off my flip-flop and slapped him as hard as I could. We began tussling, but I was no match for him. He was a 28-year old man, and I was a 13-year old girl. Size or age didn't matter to me. The only concern I had was to the safety of my younger sister. I knew that Annie wouldn't take my side, so I began running away. I ran to escape the pain and abuse I had endured. I begged and borrowed food from wherever I could. Some of my friend's parents were caring enough to let me have dinner with them on occasion. How many children have to raise themselves? How many children are actually homeless and living in the streets? The number is astronomical; far greater than the general public would care to know.

My grandparents had a strict set of rules, children were to attend school every day. Children had to be home when the street lights came on. Children did not get pregnant and bring babies home. My aunts were told that if they ever got pregnant, they were not allowed to return with their babies.

Annie could locate us from any place. Our social worker must have given her the details of our whereabouts. Annie called to plead her side of the story. She wanted us to know that the story hadn't gone down the way we were told it did. Annie stated that Greg hit her and that she needed to defend herself. As a child, I believed her story; she was my mother. For many years I believed that our state did not recognize self-defense laws. I even went so far as to ask a prosecutor about the details of Annie's case. She couldn't give me legal advice, but she made it clear that every state had a self-defense law. Annie had received a sentence of five to seven years for manslaughter. She only served a few months in prison because she was pregnant with twin boys; she was released to a half-way house for good behavior. We were pregnant at the same time. Our due dates were about a week apart.

Here I am five months pregnant with nowhere else to go. My grandparents meant well, but rules and structure were hard for me. This was one of the hardest transitions that a young person in my situation could encounter. Most people wonder why this transition would be hard for us. I felt like this was another moment of uncertainty and abandonment. When you're used to having to provide for yourself, what happens when you're no longer able? If things didn't go well with our grandparents, where would we go? We most certainly didn't know enough people here.

My grandparents were great people, but they were not ready for us. They did the best they could with two juvenile misfits. I had always been extremely attached to my grandmother. We had only visited them a few times in our lives, but her number had always been the same. If I needed to call her, I knew that I could pick up the phone and dial that number. There was always an open invitation to call her if we needed her. They lived 1900 miles away, so there was no real chance of us dropping by in a time of need. We knew that they were there, but we looked to our mother to provide for us. We hadn't ever contemplated moving away to live with her. Our mother was the only parent that we ever knew. We didn't understand this type of stability; adults that set rules and established boundaries. Adults that had high expectations without any strings attached. A roof over our heads and dinner ready every day after school. We could count on our grandparents for the support we needed.

They enrolled us in school and helped us make the transition. It was unusual getting up and going to school every day. I actually began to like it. I was making straight A's in all my classes except earth science and microbiology. I really didn't care to study rocks, dirt, and mold.

My grandmother introduced us to Jake and his family. Jake was a single father with seven children. His wife, Stephany, had been killed overseas while serving in the military. He had five boys and two girls. Jake was having a rough time dealing with his wife's death, but he was doing what he could. This was a small town, so everyone knew everyone. Grandma would stop in and check on them from time to time. She was quite close to Stephany before she passed. She had promised to help them out however she could. They were a well-rounded group given they were being raised by a single father. He worked hard to make ends meet, and the boys kept the house together. Jasmine and I became close friends with the girls Melina and Melana. We would hang out after school until about 7 p.m., then race home. We had to be home before the street lights came on.

Our new life took some getting used to, but things were changing. I seemed to be a little bored hanging out on the front stoop all day. I was increasing in size and really couldn't do much. My activity decreased over the next few months. I went from full of energy to full of belly. The days of hanging out became pretty slim. I headed straight home from school in my later months. I could only hang out on the weekends. I couldn't really do the things that everyone else was doing. I had to shift my focus from hanging out to mother mode.

I walked in the door from school, and Grandma was talking on the phone. My grandmother stayed on the phone day and night. She received a call reporting that one of her relatives was sick. She had to go out of town on short notice, so she dropped us off at my Aunt Lena's house. I was a week over my due date and terrified for her to leave. She told us to pack our bags with a week's worth of supplies. She drove us over to the trailer my aunt was staying in. I was reluctant to get out of the car. I didn't want to be left at someone else's home for a week. Plus, it was a trailer, how much room could there actually be? We knocked on the door, and my aunt let us in. Grandma spoke to Aunt Lena outside. I told her not to leave before I could talk to her. She came back in, and I rushed to the door. I stood on the front stairs, outside the trailer, begging her to take me with her. She explained that she could not take me out of town because I was due any day. I couldn't just let her leave. Why would she want to go when I needed her here? She pulled her arm away from me and said, "Nyla, I have to go!" I went inside the house and sat on the couch; I cried until I finally fell asleep.

About midnight, I woke up in excruciating pain, I had tossed and turned all night in pain. I thought I was uncomfortable from sleeping on the couch in a different place. I tried to get up and use the bathroom and then return to the couch. As the night went on, the pain grew increasingly intolerable. When the pain became too much to bear, I woke Aunt Lena up, explaining what was going on. She said, "Nyla, you're in labor."

I tried to lie on the bed and spread the creases of my buttocks. Lying on my side, rocking back and forth with my buttocks spread was the only position that relieved the pressure. Hours had passed since my labor begun. Jasmine and Dana, my cousin, stood around watching my agony. Jasmine said that it was birth control for her. I just wanted some relief from the pain. One contraction after another. I had never taken any parenting or Lamaze classes, so I didn't know what to expect. I had never even talked to anyone about the labor process. At what point do you go to the hospital? This was before the days of savvy internet information to guide you through. Although I was in pain, I couldn't help but be upset with my grandmother. She had left me in my most vulnerable hour. The emotional stress from last night's events had caused me to go into labor.

We arrived at the hospital about 8 a.m. I can hear the nurses giving the report about a 14-year old female in labor. I think I was more terrified of the judgment, I'd encounter, than the labor itself. This was a small town with a group of small minded people. All I knew was the pain I was feeling. Couldn't they give me something to take the pain away? The contractions were coming fast, but I wasn't dilated much. I felt the sudden urge to use the bathroom again. The nurses refused to let me get up and walk to the bathroom.

They said that I had to go on a bedpan, sitting on the edge of the bed, in a room full of strangers. This was so embarrassing; I had three bowel movements during the night, and now you wanted me to go, in a room full of strangers? The nursing staff reassured me that they'd take care of me. The nursing assistant cleaned me up and assisted me back to bed. The nurse then gave me some medication to help me fall asleep.

I woke up three hours later screaming! There was something trying to exit my stomach without permission. The doctor came in and checked my cervix, I was finally dilated to eight centimeters. How many more did I have to go? The doctor stuck a rod inside of me and popped my water bag. I felt a huge gush of warm fluid. The doctor said that this would help speed up the process. Indeed, it did! I felt a sudden need to get up and have another bowel movement. The nurse said, "Wait! Let us check your cervix." She urged me not to push anymore. That was a task easier said than done. She checked my cervix and said I was ready. I looked over at my aunt, like ready? Ready for what?

The nurses began pushing the bed into another room for me to give birth to my baby. The room looked like a stage scene from General Hospital. The large overhead light beamed on me as the doctor pulled his stool to the bottom of the bed. I had been in labor for 17 hours, and I didn't have enough strength to push this baby out. Aunt Lena sat at the bedside cheering me on. The doctor said that the baby's head was too large and he needed to make a small cut to assist with the pushing. One more push the nurse yelled! I mustered up all my strength and pushed as hard as I could. Out came this baby covered in a thick white substance. I yelled to the nurse, "Don't put that thing on me." I didn't have a clue what she was covered in. I didn't even know if that was normal. My beautiful daughter was born at 5:38 p.m. All the pain and struggle could not compare to the love that overwhelmed my heart. It had all been worth it! She was finally here! And she was mine!

My grandmother returned from her trip the following week, and we returned home. When Tierra turned six-weeks old, I returned to school. My grandmother had already assured me that she would not be watching Tierra while I went to school. She said that I had to find a home daycare for her. She said that she would help us out in the beginning, but Tierra was my responsibility. Initially, she gave us rides to and from the daycare, but that didn't last long.

Grandma said that I needed to be a responsible parent. This responsibility did not include her transporting us to and from school. The daycare was too far out of the way for me to walk Tierra there every morning. I would have to find another daycare for her, something that was on the route to school. I found Tierra another daycare, but the lady couldn't pronounce her name, so she called her Chocolate. She had a name, if you couldn't try and pronounce her name, then she wouldn't be back. Grandma knew a lady that did childcare, so she referred me to her. Tierra seemed quite comfortable with the lady, and she seemed to fit in, so I let her stay.

All of my high school friends were living their teenage lives. Melana and Melina were having a birthday celebration and invited Jasmine and me to come. I rarely went out, but this was at a friend's house, and I could bring Tierra. Most of the kids were from school, so it was more like a get together with music and food. Nazir had been someone that I spoke to from time to time. He didn't really show any interest in me, nor I in him. The room was packed with friends and family. We were having a great time. I was sitting on the radiator, in the living room, listening to music when Nazir walked up and asked if I wanted to dance. I was no dancer, but I graciously obliged. We danced round and round in the middle of the party. I could see the strange stares and the whispering from our friends. After the song was over, we sat in the corner and talked for hours. We didn't go to the same school, so we knew very little about each other. He knew that I had a two-month-old baby, and she was the most important thing to me. He said that he wanted to be in both our lives. He wanted to help me raise her.

Tander had been out of the picture since I left Minnesota. We had a few conversations over the phone since I had left, but that was it. I called to let him know when Tierra was born and his aunt told me that he was in jail for rape. She said that she'd give him the message when he called. I knew what Trisha had been talking about now; when she had moved away he started dating me. And he was surely with someone now that I had moved away. I didn't have hopes of getting back with him, just hopes of co-parenting our daughter.

Nazir was two years my senior and in the eleventh grade. It was close to the end of the school year, and Nazir, and I had been dating for two months. He invited me to accompany him to his junior prom. I had never been to prom before. I thought that people only attended prom their senior year. What was I going to wear? I didn't have much money, so I shopped around for an inexpensive dress.

There was a little thrift store right past the downtown area. I went into the store looking for a dress. I found the cutest purple dress with black velvet patterns on it. The dress had sleeves, but they were designed to hang off your shoulder, the middle slimmed down, and the bottom was kind of puffy. We got ready for prom at Nazir's house. Melena agreed to watch Tierra for me. Nazir's father dropped us off at the high school. We walked into the gymnasium, and the photographer was there to take pictures.

We danced and talked all night long, this was the best time I'd ever had. We left prom and walked to his cousin's house. He had a bachelor pad and let us chill. Before we had realized it, it was 6 a.m. in the morning. I just realized that I needed to get home. He walked me home, and as we approached the door, he asked if he could take me to breakfast later that morning. I didn't want our night to end, but I knew that I had to get home. I said yes to breakfast, and we kissed goodbye. I couldn't wait to see him again.

I went home and fell asleep for a few hours. I woke up around 9 a.m. and started getting ready for my breakfast date. My grandmother said that I couldn't go because I had stayed out all night. We argued over me going out to breakfast, one thing led to the other, and I was calling my aunt Lena to pick me up. Grandma said that if I couldn't abide by her rules then I needed to leave. I didn't see the issue, Nazir was a great guy, and he had a job and got good grades in school.

Aunt Lena came and picked Jasmine and me up. Jasmine didn't understand why she had to leave when she had done nothing wrong. Living with Aunt Lena was nothing like living with my grandparents. Aunt Lena was so mean, and her boyfriend was worse. Our new living situation had just gone from good to bad. My grandparents didn't give us everything, but they put a roof over our heads, we had home cooked meals, and they made sure that Tierra had what she needed. I quickly realized that I had to get a job to support my daughter because Aunt Lena wasn't going to do it. My grandmother said that Aunt Lena was getting the financial support for us and she had to supply pampers and milk for Tierra. A little incident changed the course of our lives. What did I do that had been so wrong?

Chapter 6 -
Accepting Responsibility

I have always imagined the direction I wanted my life to go. The problem was, my ideations didn't align with the decisions I made. As individuals, we tend to look for others to blame, but the truth of the matter is, we are responsible for our own destiny. Just like my mother, I had buried troves that I attempted to hide.

I got my first job, at the age of 15, working in a fast food restaurant; I was hired to operate the deep fryer. I worked in the evenings after school from 4-7 p.m. and eight-hour shifts on the weekend. My only objective was to provide for Tierra. Becoming a parent at such a young age forces you to grow up, in ways you couldn't imagine. It's one thing to take care of yourself, but the responsibility of an innocent creation is another story.

I loved being able to work and provide for my daughter. Having a paycheck of my own meant that I could buy the things that I needed. The crew was great, and so was my boss. She would put me on the schedule as long as I wanted to work. I quickly learned the deep fryer, but I was pretty bored. I sat in the back waiting for orders to be called out. I asked Linda, the manager if I could learn to operate the cash register. She looked at me in shock, and said sure! I guess she was surprised that I showed initiative. I enjoyed working and learning new things. Anytime there was an opportunity I took it.

I was smiling and cleaning the front counters when Linda approached me. She said, "I need everyone to turn in a state-issued ID card to me." I didn't have one, but I knew that if I did it would be the same outcome. Legally, you had to be 16-years old to be employed at any fast food restaurant. I lied on my application so that I could get the job.

The thoughts of dumpster diving rushed through my mind. The recollection of eating expired meals out the dumpster. The thought of never knowing where a meal was coming from shouldn't have to be any child's reality.

I explained the situation to Linda, and she said: "As much as I hate to, I have to let you go. You can reapply when you turn 16-years old, and I will make sure you get your job back."

All throughout high school, I felt like a social outcast. A wild city girl with a 4-month old baby. I tried to make the best of it, but so many unpleasant events overshadowed my primary need to provide Tierra with a stable home. It was several months before I turned 16. We would just have to make do until I could go back to work.

Nazir said that things would work out. He'd help me in any way that he could. He was working nights at a donut shop. He was 18-years old, and he was required to work. His father expected nothing less of him.

I returned to my job when I turned 16-years old. I returned as a cashier and was quickly promoted to the drive-thru. I had built a great rapport with my manager. She knew that I was a hard worker and she let me work as much as I could.

Nazir and I had gotten engaged, he proposed to me during our summer break. We had big plans to get our own place after graduation. We spent every waking moment with each other. We were together during the day when Aunt Lena was at work. At night, she made Nazir go home, but he would sneak back over.

One evening I was standing in the kitchen, and Aunt Lena came in and slapped me across my face. I was caught off guard because I didn't know what I had done. Her boyfriend had told our secret. She walked into our room, and Nazir was under my bed. Aunt Lena kicked me out of the house. A few months later, I had gotten caught in his room, and he had gotten in trouble. I had been suspended from school and kicked out of my family's home. We were now spending the night at anyone's house who would let us stay.

One afternoon, I woke up late for work after deciding to take a nap after school. I jumped up in a panic and rushed out to work. I was panicked because I had several miles to walk and no way to call my job. Walking as fast as I could, I arrived about 20 minutes late. The general manager noticed that I was clocking in after the start of my shift, so he stopped me, mid-swipe, and asked why I was late. I explained that I woke up late and had to walk to work. He offered me a three-day suspension for my tardiness, but I declined it.

I'd had enough! I exploded in my mind! Did he understand that I was homeless? A teenage parent? Had a great attendance record at work? Had a one-year-old daughter to support? That I was barely holding on to my sanity? NO, he didn't! Linda, the manager, tried to intervene on my behalf, but the GM didn't want to hear it. I was a hard worker with a great work ethic, and she knew it. I told him that I would absolutely not take the suspension. I quit on the spot! I cried all the way home. As I walked home, I had time to think about my situation. I had no home, no job and we were out of options.

This had become a continuation of the dysfunction I had known. I realized at that moment that the harder I tried the harder things seemed. My only option was to return to the streets I knew. When I made it back to the house, I told Nazir what had happened. He tried to console me, but I was past the point of comfort. I was frustrated and angry. We were sleeping at his cousin's young adult, crash pad where they partied all the time. They were a bunch of single guys, with a multitude of girls. They were young and living the young adult life. I didn't blame them, but I couldn't continue to stay there with Tierra. She was walking and into everything.

I went and picked up my last paycheck three days later. I called my best friend, Jada, to see if we could come back and stay at her house for a while. She said, "Of course." I purchased two bus tickets for the next available day. I went back to the house, packed my bags, and said my goodbyes. I told everyone that I would return once things calmed down. It turned out that we were saying goodbye for good. I had to leave Jasmine behind. She had made the transition to our new environment. Although we lived in the same home, she had teenage problems, and I was dealing with motherhood.

The decisions that we make as young adults can cause a rippling effect. Children make decisions based on feelings completely void and senseless of the future to come.

Chapter 7 -
The Long Trip Home - 1992

We loaded our bags on the bus and headed back to the big city. The ride was about 19 hours from my hometown to the big city. There was no one at the bus station to greet us; no welcoming party, no parade. We grabbed our luggage from underneath the bus and headed for the nearest bus stop. The number 23 city bus took us right in front of Jada's house. The bus let us off on the corner, diagonally, from her house.

We walked to the door and knocked, but no one was home. I started to doubt the sincerity of Jada's invitation. We sat on the front stairs watching the cars roll down the busy street. We sat outside waiting for about an hour. One by one, my friends started to arrive. We cheered and screamed as we greeted each other. It had been a long two years since I had seen them. We hadn't had any contact since I had left. Jada and Jaylen were my two best friends and had always remained consistent.

Jaylen & Jada stood in front of me, waiting to hear what had happened in Ohio. They wanted to know what had brought me back. They hadn't heard the complete story about Annie's incarceration, my living arrangements, or my engagement. I explained how Annie was locked up for manslaughter and had gotten out after having twins. She began getting high again, and the twins were taken from her. They had been placed in foster care. I excitedly told them about my engagement to Nazir and our future plans. They both were in awe and surprised at the same time. Jada asked, "What brings you back?" I explained what had happened at Aunt Lena's and Nazir's house, I had run out of places to live.

I came to the city with a total of $92 in my pocket. I asked Jada, "Can I stay for a little while until I figure things out?" Here I was in another situation. I needed to make some money and fast. I had every intention of going back, I just didn't know how or when.

My first night back, we hung out and caught up on old times. "Guys, I need to make some money" I interjected.

Jada said, "Don't worry, we got you." I had no idea what that meant, but it seemed like they were doing okay. We talked the night away, laughing and having a great time. Everyone got a chance to share what had been happening in their lives.

The next morning, I woke up early to walk down to the local fast food restaurant. The manager interviewed me on the spot and said I could start the following day. The job was working on the front line of the store, making sandwiches as the orders came in. The problem came when I actually needed to show up at work. Day in and out it was a struggle; I had to find random people in the house to leave Tierra with. When I came home at night, Jada's younger siblings complained about Tierra. They wanted to be paid for their services. I didn't have money to pay anyone because I had just started working. I made it about three weeks before I quit.

Jada and Jaylen walked in the door smiling and grinning. This time they had another friend with them, Jaime. Jaime was a short, medium size, girl that had her hair brushed into a ponytail. She stood out because she put grease in her hair and wore a bang. Our eyes instantly locked; I hadn't heard anything about her in any of our conversations. "Who is this?" I asked.

Jada responded with, "This is my home girl Jamie."

I quickly responded with, "Where did she come from?" These had been my two best friends for years, and now we had another member in the group.

I pulled Jada to the side to discuss some money affairs. I needed to know if they would let me make some money with them. We hadn't discussed what they did for money, but I had to try something. I spent the next three months on a roller coaster of madness. Jada and Jaylen introduced me to marijuana, drinking, and shoplifting. I had drunk a beer before and hit a joint, but nothing like this.

Jada took me to her room and pulled out a huge bag of weed. My eyes got big, "Where did you get that from?" I asked.

She said, "Girl we smoke, that's what we do." This life was an all-new experience for me.

We couldn't stay out past dark when I lived with my grandparents. I had never really had an interest in trying drugs. By day, we stole cartons of cigarettes and cans of baby formula, and at night we partied like teenagers. The cartons of cigarettes and cans of milk sold for $10 each. On average, we made between $100-300, dependent upon the area we hit. The money came quick, it allowed me to provide for Tierra without the stress of finding childcare. I stole our clothes, her pampers and our food while still putting a little money in my pocket. Our house was the craziest house on the block. I fell into this lifestyle head first. Years later, people still remembered us from the large gathering in front of the house.

The calls between Nazir and me had become far and few. I had started seeing other people, and so had he. This was the wildest summer of our lives. We had hit so many stores that they were on to us. Jada had developed a habit that none of us knew about. Her habit controlled what we did and how we did it. We would go into department stores and grab racks of clothes, run out with clothes on the hangers, security sensors still attached and jump in the car. She would go into stores and fill up bags full of merchandise, in front of security.

She had no regard for what lay outside of the doors. We fought the floor walkers, security guards, and anyone that tried to stop us from accomplishing our mission. Our escapades landed us in trouble on multiple occasions. We were also brought home by the police more times than I cared to count. Our summer was turning into a long list of felonies and Jada hadn't had enough. It was a miracle every time we got released from jail. The price started to be a little higher than I could afford, so I mentally began my transition out. The question still remained; what was I going to do to support Tierra? Jada would want to go out, and I would decline.

There was a car sitting in the back of the house one night and Jada invited me to come and join her. She and a friend were sitting in the parked car. As I entered the car, she introduced me to the driver. She said, "This is Yella." Yella was short for yellow because he was light skinned. They glanced at each other, and she said, "She's cool." I sat in the back seat while the two of them talked. We listened to music as he rolled up a joint.

When he lit the joint, it had a distinct smell to it. I had smoked marijuana before, but this smelled different. Jada passed the joint to me without hesitation. The joint looked and smelled funny, and the end was burning a dark brown color. The joint sizzled and popped as I inhaled it; this wasn't normal. My lips had begun to feel numb. I asked her what was different about this weed. They both glanced at each other and said, "Nothing!" I passed when she passed it to me a second time. I had this strange feeling come over me. I waited until I got out the car and ran straight to a friend of mine. I asked him had he ever smoked any weed that made him feel funny. After I described the feeling that came over me and the details of the situation, he knew exactly what I was talking about.

He said, "She had you smoking a mac."

"A mac?" I asked.

He explained that the marijuana had been laced or lined with rock cocaine. The shock and disbelief that came over my face said it all. This explained all the reckless behavior and the disregard for our safety. This information solidified for me the decision to refrain from this activity. I wanted to confront Jada about her behavior. It was one thing to choose this lifestyle for herself, but another to drag me into it. I had a strict stance on drugs because of Annie's addiction. I smoked a little marijuana, but I never wanted to be involved in anything that took me away from my daughter.

I waited for about two days until I brought the conversation up to her. I asked her why she would offer me crack without asking if I wanted to try it. She knew the struggles I had been through with Annie. She knew how disgusted I had been with our upbringing. She said that she thought I'd like it if I tried it. The truth was she wanted me to become addicted so that she wouldn't have to bear the burden alone. She pulled out a crack pipe and asked me to watch her hit it. She said that if she didn't look right smoking it, she would quit. She was 17-years old; why would anyone say that she looked good smoking a crack pipe? I could see Jada's addiction beginning to take a toll on her life. She was never at home with her girls, and she had begun stealing random things from the house.

I had a talk with Jada's mom, Lacy, later that night. She knew that she had been on some type of drugs, but she didn't know what. We talked about my future plans, and she asked me why I hadn't applied for public assistance. I honestly didn't know that was an option for me. I wasn't quite an adult; I was only 16-years old. My mind wandered back to my childhood. If these types of programs are available, why were we put out of our homes so many times? Why were the cabinets always bare? As I got older, I realized why.

I went down to the county office the very next morning and applied for cash, medical, and food stamps. I explained my situation to my intake worker, and she advised me that I'd be approved based on my circumstances. I couldn't wait to get back to the house and tell Lacy what had happened. I received the letter a couple of days later in the mail. I had qualified for $432 in cash assistance and $178 in food stamps. With this type of money, I would be able to find an apartment. The other money wasn't consistent so I couldn't consider that income. I wasn't willing to continue doing jobs to pay the bills.

Chapter 8 -
My First Apartment at 16-Years Old

I made it my mission to look for an apartment. I received a check for half the month's assistance, and I would get a full check on the first. I walked up and down the streets looking for apartments for rent. How hard could the process actually be? I walked through the neighborhood for a couple of days. I eventually found an apartment three blocks up. It was directly across the street from the park. It was a smaller apartment building that I hadn't noticed before. I had walked past it a million times in my travels. I took the number down and called it as soon as I got home. A woman answered the phone and explained the layout of the apartment. It sounded perfect! I set up an appointment to see the apartment the very next day. I skipped all the way down the street with pure excitement.

When I got to the building, I rang the doorbell. Someone buzzed me in the door, and I walked up to apartment 203. When I opened the door, the floors seemed to shine. I opened the door and entered the living room. The apartment had one bedroom, living room, dining room, bathroom, and kitchen and hardwood floors throughout. It was the best-looking apartment I had ever seen. The landlord allowed me to fill out an application. She called me back the next day and said I had gotten approved.

The only stipulation was, I had to get a co-signer. I would have to ask Lacy to co-sign for me. The landlord agreed to stop by the house the next day and speak with Lacy. After she had spoken to the landlord, she co-signed the application, and the landlord gave me my keys. I had gotten the keys to my very first apartment, and the rent was $300 a month. That was a small price to pay for peace of mind. Things had begun looking up for the first time in a long while!

Tierra and I moved into our apartment the very same day. We only brought the clothes that we had on. One of my homeboys lived on the block behind us. He donated an old bed and tv to us. On the first of the month, I walked down to the furniture store and bought Tierra a little red plastic table with two chairs. I went to the dollar store and bought some dishcloths, hand and bath towels, the essential toiletries and dishware. My homeboy spotted a little black love seat sitting in the alley, and he helped me bring it into the house. I felt like I was on top of the world. A few months of smooth sailing went by. We'd still go down to Jada's house to visit, but we didn't stay long. A few hours out and then back home.

It was a huge challenge to get the electric, gas, and telephone services in my name. Annie had these services in my name when I was younger. I had to explain that I was only sixteen and there was no possible way that I could have had these utilities prior. The stress was worth the safety and security of having my own place. This was an experience I would never let go of. A few months later a bigger apartment became available on the third floor. Tierra and I had been sharing a bedroom so I thought that she could have her own space with a larger unit. The rent was only $20 more a month. The landlord approved the transfer, so I moved my things into the larger apartment. My neighbor across the hall was moving out and gave me a wooden table with four chairs. Things continued to fall into place.

As it neared the end of summer and entered fall, Nazir and I had begun talking again. We had discussed rebuilding our relationship now that things had calmed down. He had finally graduated high school and was able to move away from home. He moved far from home to be with us. When he arrived, things weren't anything close to the way they had been. Our trust had been broken due to our infidelities. We both felt a sense of betrayal and mistrust toward one another.

He immediately started looking for a job to help with the expenses. He had always taken care of Tierra and me in the best way he knew how. All of my summer nonsense had slowly begun to catch up with me. I had racked up seven felonies ranging from joy riding in a stolen car, shoplifting, to resisting arrest.

I made sure to keep all my court appearances; my public defender arranged for house arrest since I hadn't been in trouble prior to this. Nazir got a phone line set up in his name so that I could come home. I was going to be placed under house arrest. The phone line was going to be used to monitor my ankle bracelet. The ankle bracelet transmitted a global positioning signal that pinpointed my whereabouts.

All trips and outings had to be authorized. The monitor allowed me to be in any room inside of the apartment or go outside a few feet from my home. I was allowed to go as far as the basement level. The laundry room was located down there. I couldn't remain down there for long periods of time, but I was allowed to do laundry.

Nazir and I laid on the bed watching t.v. when there was a knock on the door. I opened the door, and there stood Annie in the doorway, with her bags in hand, looking like a homeless person. I immediately asked how she got my address. She said that she had stopped by Jada's house looking for me and they informed her that I had moved. Annie needed a place to stay, so I allowed her to move in. Annie quickly became friends with the neighbors in the building. She introduced me to some of the neighbors I didn't know. I was quiet, and I kept to myself. The girl across the hall hated me, and she didn't even know me. She reported anything that happened in the building.

Annie had talked me up to one of the neighbor's brother. He came up and asked if he could talk to me. We sat in the hallway talking for hours. It was just good conversation for me. Nazir was at work, and I was on house arrest, so I was bored. Several days later he asked about me, and Annie told him that I was in the house.

He came up and knocked on the door. I invited him in to sit on the couch. As we were sitting and talking Nazir came home. He went into the bedroom and packed his bag and left. We never said a word to each other. Our relationship was already rocky, and this didn't help. The situation looked very inappropriate, but we were only talking.

The next morning, I woke up to two agents knocking on my door. I answered, puzzled. One of the officers informed me that I was under arrest. Under arrest for what? Nazir had disconnected the phone line when he left, and I had to be monitored while under house arrest. I spent the weekend in jail.

I appeared in court Monday morning. The home monitoring officer told the judge that the only reason I had been locked up was for a disconnected phone line. The judge agreed to let me go without the house arrest. I was so pissed at Nazir. Why would he disconnect the damn phone line? I didn't know where he was so I couldn't yell at him. I was so consumed with my anger toward him, I didn't see the role I played in this scenario.

I hadn't been in my new apartment a month before the landlord came knocking on the door. She left a notice that the rent hadn't been paid. I read the notice and scratched my head; "The rent hadn't been paid!" My rent was directly sent to the landlord each month by the public assistance worker. This was part of the cash assistance stipulations. My rent had to be sent directly to the landlord for the entire first year of receiving aid. I didn't have a problem with that because that's what the money was for. I called my case worker to see what had happened. She informed me that Annie had taken the liberty of going down to the county office and opening her own public assistance case. Since Tierra and I were minors, she became the legal guardian on our case. They removed me from my case and placed me under her care. She was now responsible for our well-being.

She took the money and had begun getting high again. Within weeks there was an eviction notice on the door. I was devastated! All my hard work wiped out in a matter of minutes. I screamed and yelled at her! How could she come into my home and disturb the peace I had built. We exchanged insult after insult. It was at that moment that I let her know what a horrific mother she had been all these years. After all, it was her boyfriend that had taken my innocence. I finally told her all of the things that had occurred while living in her home. How could she never have noticed the changes, the signs or symptoms of abuse? I told her that Ben had molested me from the time I was 11-years old until I was 13.

She sincerely opened her mouth to call me a liar. She said that his penis was far too big to have done the things I claimed he did. Just when I thought my level of disgust for this woman couldn't get any worse. All the volcanos in the world erupted in my head. My mind wandered back to all the moments when I had been violated by this man. All the times I had endured hurt and pain. I was at a loss for words. A person tells you something so deep and intimate, and the first reaction was that they're lying? This may have been the wrong time to bring this up, but this was not the correct response. I was infuriated and disgusted at the same time.

I realized that I needed to make some money to pay my rent. Jaylen and I came up with a plan to make some money. We decided that we were going to get into the game. We knew people who sold drugs. We had plenty of friends who we could ask. We went out and purchased a double up (a small quantity of drugs) from one of the homeboys. When people know that you're trying to make some money, they give you a little extra so you can turn a profit. Jaylen and I jumped on the bus and headed across town.

We thought we knew the perfect place to get our product off. We got off the bus and walked the streets looking for prospective buyers. We weren't as brave as we thought we were. It was embarrassing to ask people if they were crackheads. Each day we got off the bus looking for new spots. We finally ran into a block with a great deal of traffic. We thought that we had finally found the correct place to trap (make some money). We were petty drug dealers at this point. We had made enough to buy some shoes and re-up (buy another package) once or twice. Our confidence was building, and we became a little bolder. The money created a false arrogance in us.

We were standing on the corner soliciting customers when a man pulled up in a car. He waved us over to his car. He asked what we were selling. We asked what he was looking for. He said that he wanted five pills. Our eyes got big because that meant he wanted to spend $100. I opened my hand to allow him to choose which five he wanted. He grabbed the pills out of the palm of my hand. He said, "This is payment for selling on my block!" We had no clue what was going on. Apparently, he had a trap house on this block, and we were stepping on his territory. We had no business being there, but we didn't know the rules of the game. We begged him for our product back. He replied, "That's the price you pay for coming on my block." When I look back over and think through experienced eyes, the situation could have ended quite worse. Another mission failed!

I woke up the next morning feeling tired and nauseous. I didn't know if it was the stress of last night's events or a bug. I lay in the bed most of the day hoping that I'd feel better. I fell asleep for intermittent periods between the tossing and turning. I didn't feel any better the following morning, so I got up and went to the emergency room. I felt and looked green from the inside out.

I stopped by the check-in at the triage desk. The nurse asked me what brought me in. I told her that I didn't feel well and I wanted to be seen by a doctor. She asked me what my symptoms were. She took my blood pressure and temperature, but I didn't have a fever. She handed me a urine cup and instructed me to leave a sample in the window.

She said, "After you come out, get undressed, and the doctor will be in to see you." I urinated in the cup and placed it in the metallic window in the bathroom.

Shortly after I got undressed the doctor came in and said, "Do you want the good news or the bad news?" I said the bad news. He said, "You don't have a bug."

I said, "What's the good news?"

He said, "You're pregnant."

I was two months pregnant with baby number two. Nazir and I had been separated for about a month. We had been together for 18 months, and nothing happened. All of a sudden I'm pregnant, and he's gone. I knew that this changed everything. My grandmother had warned me before I left Ohio not to get pregnant again. She was so hard on me because she didn't want me to go through what she had gone through. She had two children by the time she was 18 and knew the struggles it entailed.

The minute I stepped in the door I picked up the phone to call Hank and tell him the news. I was nervous about how he was going to take it. We had only been dating a month, and I was two months pregnant. Hank seemed fine with the situation. We sat on the phone and discussed the results of my pregnancy test. Hank was the middle child of eight children.

His younger brother, Lenard, had overheard the content of our conversation. He asked Hank, "Is she pregnant again? She's only 16-years old with two children. She's a slut! Why would you want to have anything to do with her?"

Hank attempted to muffle the phone, but I had heard all the comments. Since we had been dating for such a short time, there was no strong commitment. He tried to apologize for Lenard's comments, but I had overheard every word.

I asked, "Why would my situation bother him so much?" I didn't even know who his brother was. Had I asked him or Hank to assist with my children? He knew that it wasn't his child, so he had no sense of obligation, and I was fine with that.

Hank played the dual role of husband to his mother and father to his siblings. They looked to him for guidance in their time of need. When we began dating, they perceived me as a threat to their relationships. I hadn't come into his family to take him away from his loved ones. We liked one another and wanted to see where our relationship was headed.

After receiving this news, I knew there wasn't much I could do about the apartment. I told Annie that she could keep the apartment. I packed a basket of clothes and returned to Lacy's house. In a twinkle of an eye, the carpet had been ripped out from under me. We couldn't return back to the things we had done previously so what was next? I had tried selling drugs, but it was not as easy or glamorous as the streets made it look. I found myself back in a house with no future ahead. I felt as if I was in a never ending tornado cycle!

I moped around for a few months feeling sad and depressed. Jasmine and Jamie tried to cheer me up by getting me out of the house to get some fresh air. Jasmine had her share of difficulties back in Ohio. She moved back in with our Grandparents for a short time after I left. It lasted a month or two before she was sent on a Greyhound back to Minnesota. When she arrived back in Minnesota, she lived with some of Clay's family members. We always found our way back into each other's company.

Jasmine, Jamie and I walked until we ended up on the porch of an abandoned house. Jamie was one of my newer homies, she had a mouth like nobody's business. She went to the alternative school with Jada & Jaylen. She was always ready to ride, so she could definitely rock with us. We only hung out with girls that would have our back if something went down. We decided to walk over to Jaylen's house to chill; we passed two large women sitting in their yard.

They had a child playing on the sidewalk, and when we walked past, the child called me an obscene profanity. I pushed the little kid from one side, and Jamie pushed him from the other. The two ladies came rushing to the gate yelling and screaming. I told her that her child was very disrespectful and that wouldn't be tolerated. The arguing turned into an all-out brawl. I was fighting one of the ladies, and Jamie was fighting the other. Jaylen had headed to meet us and saw the fight. She pulled the woman off of Jamie, and I continued fighting the other woman. Someone came out of the house with a bucket of bleach and attempted to douse us with the bleach. A small amount hit me in the eye. The two ladies fled to the house. We went to Jaylen's house and got cleaned up.

Jaylen asked, "What was that about?" We explained what had happened, got cleaned up and headed back to Jada's house. Jamie had proved that she was one of my ride-or-die homies.

We sat around and plotted ways to come up with some money quick. Living under someone else's roof, depending on them to feed you wasn't working. Lacy had her own children to take care of. She had helped us in every way she could. There would be food at the beginning of the month because she got food stamps, but toward the middle and end of the month, things got rough. We were at the end of the month, and the cabinets were bare. While we were talking, an older white guy rolled through the block slowly. We had noticed him creeping through the neighborhood many times; we would notice him at random times. He drove his car slowly as if he was on the prowl. We knew that he did not belong in this neighborhood.

The mark had attempted to talk to me once or twice, but I ignored him. I knew that he didn't have anything that I wanted. This time I decided to see what he had to say. He was looking for a working girl as I suspected. In this neighborhood, it could only be one of two things; sex or drugs. If he was looking for a working girl, he had to have some money to spend. The girls and I came up with a master plan to lure him back to the house. Once we had him in the house everyone would surround him and take the cash he had in his wallet.

I walked in the door, and he followed behind me. Jasmine hit him with a sharp right hook and busted his nose. Jamie followed with another right, breaking his glasses. He was discombobulated, he swayed to the left and right. Someone grabbed him by the neck and asked where the rest of his money was. He said that he didn't have anything beyond what he had in his wallet. So we came up with plan B; force him to write a check in the amount of $450. This would require someone taking him to the bank to retrieve the cash. This sounded like a good plan, but we were rookies. My homeboy Terry rode with him to the bank. Terry allowed him to go inside the bank instead of going through the drive-thru. The mark walked up to the bank teller pale and shaking. He handed the teller a check with, "Call Security" written on the back of his check.

We sat in the house pacing the floor as each hour passed. There was no sign of Terry, and we had begun to worry. What happened at the bank? As we sat on the couch discussing the list of possibilities that could have gone wrong, police officers kicked in the front and side doors. Terry had stayed in the car and "the mark" went into the bank alone. The police came looking for all parties involved in the incident. When I heard them entering, I ran to the back bedroom and hid in a large pile of clothes in the closet. Jasmine was cuffed immediately and taken to the car. They let Jamie call her mother to pick her up. They didn't find me during their initial search.

All those days of listening to Lacy complain about the boys' filthy closet had paid off. The clothes were so thick and high, the officers refused to search through them. The investigating detective called looking for me several hours later. She had questioned everyone and knew the details of the story. She gave me two options: either turn myself in voluntarily or she'd pick my daughter up for child endangerment.

I couldn't allow my daughter to be taken into foster care. I had a warrant, so she had every reason to try and entice me into turning myself in. The detective promised that if I turned myself in and answered the questions she'd let me go after my court appearance. I fell for the trap; that was most certainly not the case. Once I turned myself in, she wanted all the information on the robbery and kidnapping. DANG! Caught up again.

The gentleman painted himself as an upstanding citizen. He was a realtor by trade and stated that he was looking at properties. He pressed charges against the three of us. Jasmine took a plea deal for nine months in a juvenile facility, and my homeboy took a deal for six months. I felt the need to take my case to trial. After two months and several court appearances, while in juvenile detention, my charges were dropped. The gentleman said he had gotten enough justice with the two pleas, he didn't need to prosecute anyone else.

The whole time I was incarcerated, I explained to the public defender that he wasn't truthful with his story. He had a wife at home, and he surely didn't want her to know what he was really doing. The prosecutor and I had made a deal, regardless if I was found guilty or innocent, I would go to Juvenile Horizons. This program was designed for young women with and without children. The goal was to assist young women with life skills, teach independent living and help them return to school. I was now eight months pregnant with my second daughter, what was the worst that could happen? I really couldn't return to the situation I had come from. I was willing to give anything positive a try. I would be reunited with my daughter and out of juvenile detention before my baby was born.

Chapter 9 -
Two Children at 17-Years Old

We arrived at an old Victorian home. It wasn't anything that I had imagined. I had no expectations because this was all new to me. A facility that helped young women regain control over their lives. I knew that I had a chance to make a better life for the three of us.

Juvenile Horizons had a high school program set up on the third floor. Teachers came in and taught a regular curriculum. The daycare center was set up in the basement. Girls attended the program on a residential and non-residential basis. Some girls were bused in from home each day. There were girls from 13-17 years of age. We all have some difficulties in our past.

I met a few of the girls on the day of orientation. I was 17-years old, so I was one of the older girls. I also had a child and one on the way. Most of the girls only had one child or one on the way.

After our orientation session, we were shown to our room. We all had individual rooms. The rooms had a twin size bed, toddler bed, and a crib for the baby.

The bathroom was located outside my room. There was a common area to watch television and attend meetings. The kitchen was located in the basement. There was a cook on site to prepare breakfast, lunch, and dinner. The purpose of the program was to teach us parenting skills. We attended school on the third floor, and the child care center was in the basement. The director set up accounts to ensure we were budgeting our money.

I was only in the program for a few weeks before I gave birth to my baby girl. This pregnancy was very sensitive, anything strenuous caused me to have contractions. I had sex prior to arriving and had been in labor intermittently for weeks. The contractions were so bad I thought that I was going to have her any minute.

The contractions had been on and off for the first few weeks. One of the girls told me to take Castor Oil to induce my labor. She said that it was guaranteed to work. I was only eight months; the baby should be fine right? I was in so much pain that I would be willing to try anything at this point.

The younger girls looked up to me. I mentioned Jada, and they told me all about her stay. She was getting high the whole time she was in the program. Her stay didn't last long because she got kicked out.

I talked to Hank every night before I went to bed. We spent almost every day together before I went to the juvenile detention center. I walked two miles to and from his house each day. He did a great job of hiding his feelings for me. I knew he liked me, but I didn't really know how much. I enjoyed spending every moment with him.

He was the kind of guy I was looking for. He had a great amount of confidence that was borderline arrogance. He loved to dress in the best clothes. He was a role model for any young man looking to be hood rich. Urban slang defines hood rich as someone who lives in a poor area, but dresses nice, drives a luxury car and lives at home with their mother. His friends and family members looked up to him.

After I got off the phone, I took a cap full of the Castor Oil and headed to bed. I fell asleep relatively quick but woke up about three hours later in severe pain. I looked over at the clock to see what time it was. I wanted to calculate how long it actually took for the Castor Oil to work.

My contractions were intense, and they had increased in frequency. I began timing them after I woke up. They were about five minutes apart. My first thoughts were; I'm going to have this baby any minute. I called Maria, the night shift staff member, for help. They had a protocol in place for this type of thing. Maria called the person on call for assistance. Chelsea was on call, so she was designated to take me to the hospital.

I had packed my overnight bag in preparation for my delivery. I began gathering our belongings for the hospitalization. Chelsea pulled up to the front door, and Maria came to my room to let me know that she was there. Chelsea drove me to Hennepin County Medical Center where I saw my OB/GYN. She wasn't required to stay with me, nor make sure that I was admitted. Tierra and I got out of the car and headed into the emergency room. I couldn't leave Tierra with any of the girls at the residence. It was against the rules, so I had to take her with me. I called Hank and Lacy (Jada's mother) to let them know I was in labor and headed to the hospital.

Upon arrival, the doctor came in and assessed me. He found that my baby was breach. I was only 32 weeks, and she hadn't had time to position herself head down. The nurses tucked Tierra and me in the bed. She knew that it was going to be a long night. The baby wasn't in any distress, so she assisted in making me comfortable. She gave me pain meds to control the pain. Once the pain went away, I fell asleep with Tierra snuggled beside me.

The doctor knew that I'd probably require a C-section because of the baby's position. Before I went to sleep, I called Hank to update him on the situation. He said that the buses had stopped running and he wouldn't be able to get there until after 5 a.m. I prayed that nothing happened before he got there. I woke up to a team of doctors at my bedside. Two doctors tried to manually turn the baby from the outside, but they were unsuccessful. They had scheduled the surgery for 9 a.m. That gave Hank and Lacy plenty of time to get to the hospital.

Tierra was three years old and didn't care for Hank. When he would spend the night, she would pee on his clothes. Other times, she would hide articles of his clothing. They didn't really know each other, but he was the only person I could trust to watch over her. He finally arrived about 6 a.m. and took her to his family's house. I have always been an overprotective mother. Trusting people with my children didn't come naturally to me. I had no choice, I had to focus on my unborn child.

Ria was born at 9:51 a.m. that morning. She had straight black hair, brown skin, and a round face. I was now the mother of two beautiful girls. I was also a 17-year old girl that had no idea how to be a woman, let alone, mother the two adult responsibilities I now had. I stayed in the hospital for four days after having surgery. Hank said that his experience with Tierra had been quite successful. He said that he filled her pockets with candy and they became the best of friends.

We returned to the JH after I was released from the hospital. Participation in the program increased our incentives outside of the program. One of the incentives was the use of a weekend pass for those that had somewhere to go. I used Lacy's residence on my home address, so I could go spend the weekend with Hank.

I packed up both children on Friday evenings, and we headed out. Our weekend gear included a stroller, a duffle bag, diaper bag, and the walker. Tierra would ride in the stroller and Ria was in the carrier on my stomach. Our bags would drape off either side of the stroller. It was an ordeal to get across town for those weekend passes, but it was worth spending time with Hank and being away from the residence.

The first weekend out was spent at Lacy's house. Hank and I sat on the couch and talked while Jaylen and Aaron, a longtime friend of ours, were on the other couch joking around. I overheard the conversation, so I jumped in with a few remarks; we had all been friends for years. We always joked around and gave each other a hard time. That was the very nature of our relationship. Nothing in our behavior had changed this day.

Aaron jumped up and rushed out the door. He quickly returned with two other guys carrying guns. They walked into the house and started pointing the guns, "Who's in here talking crazy?" The incident had occurred between Jaylen & me, and when they turned they suspected it was Hank. He had no idea what was going on. He had seen the guys come in the house with their guns drawn and began making his way to the door. As he was trying to exit, he had a scuffle with the guy at the door. The guy refused to let him out, so he had to fight his way out. As they tussled, the other guy pulled his gun out and started shooting. I ran toward the bedroom where the kids were.

My 3-week old baby was laying on the bed, and Tierra was playing on the floor. I grabbed both of them and hid in the closet. They shot up the entire house. I could hear gunshot after gunshot. I prayed that Hank was okay. I didn't know what had happened to Jaylen. She was standing in the living room exchanging words with both men before the shooting started. Everyone in the house ran and took shelter. We sat there as gunshot after gunshot rang out. I couldn't even understand how this escalated so quickly. A few friends sitting around laughing and joking and now we're in a closet hiding for our lives. After the gunshots stopped, I quietly tiptoed to the bedroom door.

I opened the door to see if anyone was still in the house. The living room was clear, the doors were wide open, and the walls were riddled with bullet holes. I looked outside to make sure Hank wasn't out there laying on the ground. I later got word that he had been shot in the arm. Lenard said that he had been shot in his arm. His father lived a few blocks away, so he ran to his house.

The shooting caused a ripple effect; Hank wanted to know who the shooters were so that he could retaliate. His family had several questions about my role in the shooting. I didn't have answers for any of them because honestly, there was no role. Jaylen hadn't done anything, and neither had I. I didn't know either of the men that came to the door. We all had a friendship with Aaron because we had all gone to high school together.

This house had seen more than its share of incidents. There were six teenagers that knew everyone in the neighborhood. We knew everyone, and everyone knew us (including those we didn't know). Our house was the place for all the children to come hang out. We chilled on the front stairs all summer long without any events. It wasn't until we communed with outsiders that these atypical incidents occurred.

After all the drama, we still had to return to JH that Sunday evening. It was hard to return knowing what had happened this weekend. I was uncertain about Hank's physical and mental state. I hadn't really seen or heard from him since the altercation, and we had to go back.

Hank finally called when I made it back to JH. He explained what happened and how he made it to his father's home. We decided to change our home visits for the next few months. I was more afraid that he would blame me for the incident because it happened at my home. I did everything I needed to do to complete the program.

Hank and I had decided to move past the altercation and continue working on our relationship. He would never stay another night at Lacy's house, so we stayed in hotels or at his mother's house when we came home. We planned on getting an apartment together once I graduated from the program.

In the short six months that we were in the program, we had developed some relationships. Each of us was on our own journey in life. We were all from broken homes and looked forward to raising our children. We were young women that didn't know much about life. Most of the young women in the program were from different parts of the metro area. Our relationships didn't go beyond the walls of the facility.

The counselors invited us to attend the outpatient program, but I declined. I wanted to start fresh with my new found stability. This was a second chance for me. I wanted to maintain my family and raise my children. So I pressed forward to the next part of my journey.

Chapter 10 -
Free to Be Me at 17-Years Old!

We had completed our court recommended, six-month length of stay. Tierra and I had a social worker designated to help with any available county funding. He assisted us with a clothing voucher, resources in the community for household goods, and a voucher for furniture. We had utilized every resource he offered us. I found an apartment a block over from my very first apartment. I found a two-bedroom apartment, in a four-plex building, in a fairly rough neighborhood.

Hank and I moved in together; it was the typical teenage crash pad. All our friends came over to hang out most of the time. Our first fight in the apartment disturbed the whole complex. Hank had got a gun after the shooting. We were arguing, I grabbed the gun and threw it out the door. The gun went right through the neighbor's passenger window. We shifted the arguing from us to them. I attempted to apologize, but the lady didn't want to hear it. She demanded that I pay for her replacement window. It was only right, but I don't take kindly to demand. I refused to pay for it. The neighbors never really spoke to me again.

Our apartment was full of summer time fun and partying. Hank ran the streets all day and night, and I hung out with my friends. Hank and I hadn't ever lived together, so I didn't really know this side of him. Annie and her new found girlfriend showed up on my doorsteps again. She moved into the apartment upstairs. The landlord really didn't care who rented the apartments as long as they got their rent. Annie allowed some of our homeboys to sell drugs out of her apartment.

We watched as the decent neighbors moved out and the drug addicts moved in. I hadn't re-enrolled in school since I left JH. All my friends had dropped out, and I thought that I would be missing something if I attended school. Smoking weed and drinking daily got old quick. Our younger friends would come over and graffiti the walls. The landlord said that we had to clean it up or we would be evicted. Teenage delinquents running in and out of the front and back doors.

Hank was a great hustler, he taught me all I needed to know about the streets. I felt that we were a match made for each other. If anything went down, I could always count on him to have my back, and I'd have his. This was the life for me! Then I woke up!

In urban culture, gang affiliation is acceptable for those that need a sense of belonging. Young men that grow up in a fatherless home have a sense or need to feel like they are a part of something. Gang affiliation started off as an organization, a place for young men to feel they had somewhere to turn. Over the years, the culture has changed. Hank grew up feeling like he needed to belong to something, so he joined. Some of his friends were members of the same organization.

Chapter 11 -
My Reality Check at 19-Years Old

It was time to reevaluate my priorities in life; Hank was constantly cheating, and I had no career path. To make matters worse, we had both dropped out of high school. Hank's mother, Bridgette, was supportive of us going to school. One of the stipulations to receiving cash assistance was work reform. In 1996, the Clinton Administration placed strict rules on people receiving assistance. Recipients had to either go to school or look for a 40-hour a week job. I decided that I needed to go back to school. My case worker helped me find programs that provided alternative forms of education. I enrolled in a full-time G.E.D. program. Bridgette provided childcare while I attended school. It was more like drop your baby off in front of the tv care.

Bridgette had aspiring dreams for her son. She wanted him to be the biggest drug dealer on this side of the city. She would help him get on (buy drugs), then ask for money to pay the bills. He was more of a husband figure than a son. When we first started dating, he talked to her about me. He told her how he felt and she gave her opinion of me. She approved of me as a person, but I wasn't the "type" of woman she imagined him with. He was above me and deserved to be with the supermodel chic.

Those seeds had been planted from day one, so that's the type of women he looked for. He said that when he was cheating, he was always looking for better; better meaning, someone greater than me. Of course, I didn't know any of this then; it would be 20 years later before he opened up about this. Time flies when you're chasing your tail. All I knew was I loved this man, and he didn't seem satisfied with me. I constantly did things to improve my appearance, but that was not the answer. My self-esteem was very low.

I always wondered why he came back if I wasn't good enough. The truth was he couldn't live up to the street code and be honest with himself. He wanted to be everything that everyone called him to be. The more women you sleep with the "more" of a man you are. He enjoyed the attention. He also listened to his mother's false ideations instead of following his heart.

I realized that I had been giving the greatest part of me away; my heart! I had allowed people, especially men, to misuse and abuse me. I endured domestic violence in several relationships. Hank once told me that if someone loves you, they'll show it. Love was an action word, and a man will provide it in his actions. Being in a relationship and having sex with someone is not the meaning of love.

When a person loves you, they will treasure you. Hank and I were in a seven-year relationship; he cheated on me every time he got mad at me. I know this because he told me. I can't even explain how often that was. He would make up things to argue about just so he could stay in the streets. Then he'd come back and confess how much he loved me and we'd work it out. I believed that regardless of who he had been with, he still loved me! Talk about blind, ignorant, and arrogant. We had a connection like no one I'd ever been with. We could sit and talk for hours. The true art of loving a woman is intimacy; true communication. Two people allowing themselves to be vulnerable and honest with one another. We would pour out our feelings, mine more than his. The bond we shared was deeply rooted. We both came from dysfunctional backgrounds; raised in a world of drug addicted parents. Both of our mothers had been victimized in their childhood and lacked any real growth after bearing children. In our community, it is taboo to speak of the things that happened to you as a child.

Young women are molested and abused by close relatives, but yet their mothers never know. How is it that women of similar circumstances encounter the same tragedy but fail to identify the signs? It's a vicious cycle of victimization that takes place in far too many families. It creates a cycle of shame and low self-esteem in the women that were meant to be more than this.

Most women are unable to talk about it, so counseling is never considered an option. Women, especially African American women, do not talk to people about things of this nature, we just bury it and move on. I know more women in my community who have been victims of child molestation, rape, and domestic abuse, than those that have graduated from high school. Our parents turned to drugs to coat the pain and hide their shame.

People do not understand the physical, psychological, or emotional connection with drug abuse nor the why. The why behind recreational drug use and physical dependence of drug addiction. As a child, I would often wonder why my mother and father wouldn't stop using drugs. Why they couldn't manage their finances or prepare us a meal? The truth is, most people just can't do it alone! They must first acknowledge the problem, then seek the solution. At the end of every stem, there is a root. If you follow the trail, you'll surely get to the bottom.

Hank and I wanted to take on the world together. He and his family were all I had. Every birthday, holiday, or event we spent together. They had replaced my maternal and paternal family. We got married, for the first time, at 20-years old. He was incarcerated, but they allowed inmates to get married at the courthouse.

After I had Ria, Hank proposed to me. We were going through the drive-thru at McDonald's, and he handed me an engagement ring. The ring had a solid, small diamond in it. He said that he had bought the ring and wanted to give it to me. He was kind of nonchalant when he passed the ring to me. He wasn't ever one to profess his love. He hid his emotions well. I always felt like he truly loved me, but didn't know how to express it. His feelings would be perceived as a sign of weakness if he actually showed them. He was a different person when we were at home versus the person he portrayed in the streets.

The first time he proposed we were 17-years old. I had given the ring back many years ago in the midst of a fight. He cheated so often, I couldn't believe that he actually wanted to get married. I wondered if his proposal was sincere. What happened to those two teenagers that were madly in love with one another? I always stuck by him in hopes that things would get better.

When he was sentenced to three years in prison, I decided to stick by him. I had waited for him before so this would be no different. We were two broken people, seeking the love we had never gotten from our parents. He was there for me when I thought that I had no one else. I was broken, and he tried to fix me. Men have a funny way of expressing themselves, sometimes. He wanted to be my savior, but he also needed to be saved. I believed that if we stuck together, we could conquer the world together. We were in love with the ideation of the loyalty we shared. Loyalty and love can be confused when you don't know the difference. I thought that we were soul mates. God had brought us together to make each other better, but instead, we destroyed one another.

Prior to Hank's incarceration, I graduated with my G.E.D. Now that he was going away, I decided to continue on to college. I chose a degree in accounting because I was great in math. The accounting program would take a total of 24 months to obtain a degree if I attended school full time. I made it to the second semester before I decided that this wasn't for me. I needed a shorter program that would help me get into the workforce. Two years was too long to be attending school and hustling on the side.

Bridgette always told grandiose stories about the healthcare field and its financial benefits. She had been a medical assistant for 20 years, and she loved taking care of people. She could work for temporary agencies on a daily basis and make the money she needed. She used the money to get high. She reminded me of Annie because they moved around a lot. Bridgette spent most of her money getting high just as Annie did. Bridgette always kept a place for a short amount of time. She would go months without paying the landlord before they evicted her.

Hank and his siblings never experienced the foster system, but he knew what it was like to be homeless. The feeling of waking up with the sheriff standing over your head, telling you to grab your things. I didn't envy that part of his life at all. It reminded me of my childhood with Annie. Our lives shadowed one another's in various areas. We sympathized with one another because we had similar struggles.

I was intrigued by the stories that Bridgette told and wanted to see what healthcare had to offer me. Hank had other family members that were nursing assistants, so I decided to try that career path.

I enrolled myself in a two-week training program to become a nursing assistant instead. The nursing home taught classes on site followed by three months of on the job training. This route seemed more lucrative, the program was short, and I could begin working sooner. I wanted to work in a healthcare field that had flexible hours and various locations.

I quickly discovered that this part of the healthcare field was not as glorious as other healthcare providers had claimed. I worked shift after shift, trying to make the type of money Bridgette had promised. My first job was at a nursing home, making $7.25 an hour, working 11pm-7am. I worked full time at 72 hours a pay period. Immediately after I got out of orientation, I began picking up extra shifts. I picked up four extra eight-hour shifts, working 3-11pm on the days I already worked. I was so excited because I had worked enough extra shifts to finally make some decent money.

Payday was finally here, I rushed in full of excitement to pick up my check. I opened my check and read that it was a whole $688 after taxes. My mouth dropped open in disappointment. I had to take three buses to get to work and three buses home. I took a bus to drop my children off at daycare, then two buses to get to the job. Caring for elderly people that required total assistance with everything was very difficult.

My mind quickly reverted to my old ways. I could make this money in a few hours on the block. I had to remind myself that I had changed my lifestyle to provide my daughters with a better future. They couldn't have two parents in jail. Hank was in jail, and it was time for me to move away from the inner city. It was too easy for me to go back to my old ways. I needed to place some distance between me and the old neighborhood.

Plus, so many things had happened over the course of the years. There is a certain amount of danger that comes with living the street life. We had experienced several of the drawbacks. We had been robbed at gunpoint, my house was broken into, and I had been raided by the police. The person that robbed my house was one of my clients. He had been up all night getting high. He was known for breaking and entering. He had sold me his wife's radio while she was sleeping. When she woke up, he was instructed to go get it back. He climbed through my bedroom window and took back the things he had sold me, plus some of my things. I knew that it was time to move away.

I moved into an upstairs apartment across town to get out of the neighborhood. The landlord was a creep. The couple downstairs didn't have any problems out of him because they had a man around. He knew that I was single with two children, so he did things that were illegal. He would show up at all times, for no apparent reason. He would enter my apartment whether I was home or not. I sat on the couch one Saturday afternoon and deliberately didn't answer the door. He used his key and came in. When he opened the door, I was sitting there looking at him. He had his sons with him and asked why I didn't open the door. I asked him why he didn't call before he decided to come over. He didn't have a response, so I said that's why I didn't open the door. You need to call before you just show up at my place. After I confronted him about invading my privacy, he would do all kinds of things to make me uncomfortable. He started calling before he came, but I wouldn't answer. Then I started taking the phone off the hook when I wasn't home. He caught on to that very quickly.

He went so far as to disconnect my lights from the basement knowing that I didn't have access to it. The downstairs neighbors were the only ones with access to the basement. The children and I would go days without lights. All the food in the refrigerator spoiled. I finally went downstairs and talked to the neighbors about checking the breaker box. He went downstairs and flipped the switch for me and the lights came back on. I tried calling the owner, but he acted as if he didn't have anything to do with all the things that were happening in my apartment.

I was trying to start my life on a better note, but things just kept happening to me. I did manage to scrape up the money for my first car. I went to the auction and won a red four-door Honda. All cars were bought as is. After I paid for the car, I could get in and check it out. I paid the $400 at the impound window. I got the keys in hand and ran out to get in the car. I placed the key in the ignition, and the car wouldn't start.

I was bummed out; I had bought a car that didn't run. I had to figure out how I was going to get the car home. I had it towed to my apartment for an extra $40. I let the car sit in the back of my house for a few days before doing anything with it. I was still taking the bus to and from work. I knocked on the neighbor's door and asked to speak to her husband. I had seen him working on their car, so I asked what he thought the problem could be. He suggested that I take the battery out and walk it down the street to the automotive garage. I walked it up there and asked if they could charge the battery for me.

The mechanic said that he'd take a look at it and call me later. I hoped that it was something as simple as a battery. I walked home so I could take a nap before work. I was awakened by the telephone ringing. The mechanic said that the battery was frozen solid. He had to let the battery defrost before he could charge it. Minnesota has some very low wind chills during the winter. I was excited to hear that the battery was the problem. I couldn't walk up to the shop right then because I had to get ready for work. It took me about two hours on the bus, so I had to head out soon. I would walk up to the garage after I got off work in the morning. I walked up to the garage midafternoon, as anticipated.

I paid for the battery repair and headed home. I put the battery in the car and the car still didn't start. Dang it! I went into the house and asked my neighbor if he could jump my car. He came out and jump started my car, and it started up! I was so excited, no more riding the bus in the dead of winter. I had been really rolling the dice by leaving Tierra and Ria home alone at night. I tried to make sure that they were sleep before I left, but they were just faking it. Thank God for grace and mercy! Looking back at it, anything could have happened to them, and no one would have known where I was.

Jasmine and I had connected again, and we decided to move in together. She was in need of a place, and I needed to get out of this apartment. One of my friend's parents had just bought a bigger house, and she was looking to rent her old home. She told us that it would be a little more expensive than the apartment I was renting. It was not because Jasmine and I would be sharing the bills. Within a week Jasmine and Sharon had helped me move out of this place. The landlord filed a civil judgment on me because I broke the lease, but I didn't care.

I believe that was his intention all along. I learned a valuable lesson in the situation. Sometimes we are busy trying to get what somebody has to offer, but instead, we should be investigating them and what they're trying to offer. How many other tenants had he done this to? That apartment should have come with a warning label, "Crazy landlord looking for a tenant!"

Jasmine and I moved into our little house on the hill. It was a two-bedroom with a kitchen, living room, and screened-in back porch. It was very small, but we made it our own. Jasmine loved cooking, so she took control of the kitchen. The kitchen was too small for me, so I barely went in there. My favorite room was the living room. It was really nice to have someone around to help me with the kids. We shared all the expenses, and things were lovely. She worked during the day, and I worked at night initially.

I enrolled Ria in pre-school two days a week so I could get some sleep during the day. She had tried to make herself some toast in the microwave and put the timer on 10 minutes. She burnt the toast and filled the house full of smoke. I knew that she was getting older and wouldn't just stay in the room while I was sleeping. Tierra was in kindergarten, so she was gone during the day. I would usually wake up before she got home from school so I could spend some time with her before going to work.

Two and a half years went by, and Hank and I had separated. I loved him but didn't believe that he was going to get out of jail and do all the things he promised. He didn't understand what happened to make me have a change of heart. I knew that he would say all the right things while he was locked up, then do the complete opposite when he got out. I loved having him all to myself, but what was going to happen when he was able to do what he wanted. I let fear grip my heart and ended the relationship six months prior to him getting out of jail. Hank got out of jail and moved in with his mother. I didn't tell him the complete and honest truth, but I had been on a few dates with Jeremy.

To Hank's surprise, I had become pregnant while he was incarcerated. I was 23-years old when I had my first son. My son was the best thing that came out of this relationship. Jeremy, my son's father, was an abusive, alcoholic who always wanted to measure up to Hank. Jeremy was the type of person who liked to party and have fun. He didn't have any sense of responsibility. He caught me at a very vulnerable time in my life. I just wanted to hang out and have a good time, but ended up being stuck with him. He was a good conversationalist and had a knack for charming women. Nine months later I gave birth to a beautiful baby boy.

My son was born at 8-pounds and 13-ounces. He was hypoglycemic when he was born, so he was required to spend time in the newborn intensive care unit. He spent the first three weeks of his life in the NICU. My son was the cutest, little chunky boy I'd ever seen. He was light-skinned with a head full of curly hair. He looked like a mini football player. I wondered if God was punishing me for leaving my husband while he was in prison. Through a lot of prayer and education, I learned that God is loving, He doesn't punish people for their decisions. Your decisions have their own consequences. Nevertheless, my son was a gift from heaven, and I was just praying that he was going to be alright. They never found what caused the hypoglycemia. He came home after making a full recovery.

Jeremy and I weren't a good couple. I worked, and he dated Jasmine's friends. He found it to be a challenge to sleep with women we said he had no chance with. This caused some tension between Jasmine and me because I didn't understand how her friends could come over and sit at my house, then hang out with Jeremy at night. Jasmine was stuck in the middle of all this drama. She had been friends with these women for many years, and I was her sister.

Jeremy claimed that he wasn't doing anything with any of them, but I knew he was. I tried to work things out for the sake of my son, but it really wasn't worth it. I stayed and tried to make the best out of it. He came and went how he pleased, and I really didn't mind. He was an alcoholic and spent most of his time drinking. As long as he watched Xavier during the day, he could do what he wanted at night. One of the girls claimed to be pregnant by him. I didn't know what they expected from him or me; he didn't take care of the only child he had. I guess I hadn't learned my lesson the first time around. Jeremy hadn't changed, he was the same person, just older and more experienced.

As if there wasn't enough drama going on, we received a letter in the mail stating that we needed to vacate the property by the end of the month. Sharon had been diagnosed with cancer and couldn't afford to pay the mortgage on both homes anymore. She was still working while she was receiving chemotherapy. I sympathized with her, but this was no way for us to find out. Jasmine and I had been paying our rent, but she was not paying the mortgage on this house.

I called down to the county to talk to the person that had sent the letter out. I explained to him that I had a newborn baby and two other children. We couldn't find a place on such short notice. He gave me an extension on the deadline, but in the meantime, the water had been shut off. The water bill hadn't been paid for several months either. Sharon was responsible for all these bills. I called her, but she wouldn't answer. If she had told us what was going on, we could have paid our own bills.

We were forced to move back to the north side of town. We quickly found a two-bedroom duplex. It was much larger than our little house, but the rent was a little more expensive. Jasmine's friend had gotten me a job at the dispatch center before I found out she was sleeping with Jeremy. It was a well thought out plan because she would be on one line talking to him while I was sitting across the room working.

She knew what hours I worked and what days I had off. I would come home sometimes, and she'd already be at my house. They claimed to be friends, so I ignored the intuition in my gut. They had also tried to throw me off their trail by telling me that she was sleeping with Jeremy's brother. He had a girlfriend, but he had the same morals and values.

After a long day at work, I walked into the house to hear the phone ringing. As I looked at the phone, it was ringing in slow motion. Jeremy looked at me and went out the back door. His routine was to leave as soon as I got home. Our eyes locked as he walked past me and he closed the back door. The phone was ringing as if I could see the urgency of the call.

There was something about the way that Jeremy looked at me when he left that had stuck with me. I turned to reach over and pick up the phone. I answered it, "Hello?"

My ex-sister-in-law was on the phone hysterically crying. She said, "I've been calling all day, haven't you gotten any of my messages?" This was before cell phones had become so popular.

Jeremy had deliberately neglected to tell me she had been calling all day. Now I understood the sneakiness in his eyes. He had contempt for Hank and his family. He didn't want me to have anything to do with him or his family. Hank and I still had a cordial relationship for our daughter's sake, and he was a better friend than a lover. They had been my family for years, so I wasn't just going to cut off all communication with them because I wasn't with him.

I asked, "What's going on?"

She responded with, "Hank got shot, and they don't know if he's going to make it!"

I said, "WHAT are you talking about? I need you to explain to me what happened to him." As she was describing the details of the story, I could relate to the sense of urgency in her voice. He had been headed home from one of his trap houses and ran into someone he had a beef with. The guy pulled out a gun, and Hank pulled out his.

They ended up in a shootout, but only Hank was hit. He had been shot in the butt with a .22 caliber bullet and it traveled up through his abdomen. It is said that this caliber is the most dangerous because it can cause internal damage. I asked her what hospital she was at and grabbed my keys. I told her that I was on my way to the hospital and I would see her shortly. When the paramedics brought him into the emergency room, they immediately rushed him into surgery.

The doctors said that they couldn't give the family any updates on his status until they opened him up and explored the damage. Hank and I remained friends and co-parents after the break-up. He had a new family and had my little family as well.

So back to the story; I arrived at the hospital to see how Hank was doing. I wasn't welcomed by his current girlfriend or the band of hood rats by her side. I pushed past them and listened as they made their remarks. I had the girls with me just in case the situation was as grave as reported. I walked into the room to find him lying in bed with a nasogastric tube down his nose. He had a large bandage on his abdomen. He was lethargic but responsive. I let out a huge sigh of relief knowing that he was still alive. I stood by his bed and told him not to ever scare me like that again!

I spent each evening at the hospital after work. I still had some fear of losing my dear friend. After the third night of being at the hospital, I went home, walked in the door and went straight to the bed. I was exhausted from working all day and being at the hospital at night. Jeremy walked in the door shortly after I had laid down, in a drunken stupor. He said that he had been trying to call me but my cell phone was off. I had gotten a cell phone after this incident. He would call non-stop when he thought I was at the hospital, so I began turning it off when I entered the building. I tried leaving it in my car, but that didn't work either; he would just call repeatedly. His demeanor was that of a drunk and agitated man. He loved to pick a fight when he had been out drinking. He drank every night, and we fought quite often. Our fights had been bad before, but this time was the worst. He accused me of being in love with Hank.

The truth was, I did love Hank. We weren't together, and I was trying to move on with my life, but that didn't change how I felt about him. I never wanted anything bad to happen to him just because we didn't work out. He may have been better suited for another woman. I replied with, "You could never be half the man he is!" I was tired of defending our relationship to him! He was a great father to our children and a great friend to me, but why did I say that to this man?

Never antagonize the devil or an insecure man for that matter. He turned and pulled all the phones cords out of the walls. He charged at me and drug me out of bed. He drug me into the living room away from my sleeping son and beat the crap out of me. He punched me so hard, in my mouth that I could feel my teeth go through my lip.

My mouth instantly began to swell. He grabbed me by my neck and held me to the ground. He laid all of his 300 pounds on my back as he choked me; 300 pounds of hate and anger. I could see my life flash before my eyes. I just knew that he was going to kill me. I screamed for help, but the neighbors never responded. As I was about to pass out, he let my neck go.

My son was about six months old now. He was in the bedroom fast asleep under the covers. He never woke up once through all the screaming. After Jeremy let go of my neck, I laid down on the floor for a few more minutes. I was terrified to move, but I didn't want to stay down on the floor for too long. I got up off the floor and rushed into the kitchen. He grabbed a knife from the kitchen drawer and threatened to kill me with it. He paced the floor, threatening to kill me for hours.

He was a smoker and chain-smoked as he paced the floor. I stood by and all night contemplated ways to escape. I couldn't figure out how I was going to get my son from the bedroom, then get out the back door. None of the scenarios ended with me saving us both. There were too many factors. The room way too far from the back door. I imagined racing to the door and running for my car. Jasmine had gotten her own apartment right up the street. If I could only make it there! My car was a stick shift so there would be too much of a time lapse between getting to my car, unlocking the doors, getting the keys in the ignition and getting it into gear.

The parking lot was on a downward slope also. So just putting it into gear and backing up took too much time. Several hours went past, and I was physically and mentally exhausted. I couldn't leave my son because I didn't know what Jeremy was capable of. I finally began to pray; I had been saved years back so I knew prayer would help. I felt so much shame for ruining my marriage and hooking up with this man that I stopped going to church. It didn't matter what Hank had done prior to our marriage, I had made a commitment to start a new life with him. My betrayal with Jeremy ruined that. I felt that everyone at church would know what happened and be less forgiving.

I couldn't come up with a scenario that would work for us, so I walked to my room and laid down. I figured that if Jeremy was going to kill me, there was nothing I could do about it. He had held me at knife point for six hours before he let up. My usual routine was to pick up Jasmine for work in the morning. I would drop her off at work and then continue to my job. When I didn't show up that morning, she took a cab to my house.

She walked in the door and took one look at me and knew what had happened. I was just thankful that I was still alive. I almost gave my life for his; Jeremy almost took my life because I was defending Hank. She took my car and said that she would be back after work. Jeremy had left once she arrived. I could see the disappointment and anger all over her face. She had moved out because she was tired of the arguing and fighting. I was thankful that the girls weren't home either.

Later that morning, there was a knock on the door. I was hesitant about opening the door because I didn't know who it could be. Hank and his sister, Tesha, coincidentally stopped by to check on me. He had been released from the hospital and was doing much better. He said that he had a feeling that something was wrong with me. There had been several incidents where we both just had an overwhelming feeling that something was wrong with one another. Many of the times it was true; something was always going on in one of our lives.

I sat at the table with my mouth swollen shut and tears running down my face. Jeremy was the man that I had allowed to ruin our relationship, and Hank was still consoling me. Hank tried to tell me that it wasn't my fault, but I was filled with shame. I questioned my moral judgment and reasoning. Why couldn't our relationship have worked out? Hank hated to see someone else inflict pain on me. He reached into his waistband and gave me his gun. He said that I should use it for protection. Then, he told me to call him if I needed anything.

Taking the gun gave me an ounce of security. It truly didn't help because I woke up two days later to Jeremy standing over me pointing a gun in my face. He just wanted to let me know that he could get to me anytime. The kids would go outside and play, leaving the doors unlocked. He would walk in at any moment to harass me. After a few days had passed, he called and asked if I would come to his Aunt's house.

I don't know why I did it, but I did. I wasn't there five minutes before we got into a huge argument. I left out the door, and he chased after me. He tried to kick me down a flight of concrete stairs, but I guided my body toward the grass. There were 22 stairs in all, and he tried to make sure that I hurt myself.

I ended up rolling down the hill and scraping up my entire left arm. I couldn't stop to examine it, I had to get to my car because he was still charging after me. I made it to my car, and as I was driving off I call him a fat bastard! He lifted his leg and kicked my driver window in. He was trying to grab me out of the car. I sped off with his arms in the car.

I turned around at the corner and came charging down the street. I was pissed at this point. I came flying as fast as I could; I tried to hit his big behind with my car. I missed him, but that didn't stop the thoughts. I was tired of being abused by this man. I sat at the stop sign contemplating if I should turn around and go back. I didn't want to chance it. What if he got close to me this time? I pulled off and headed home. When I walked in the door, I stopped to assess the damages to my arm. I had a large abrasion from my wrist to the elbow. I cleaned all the grass and debris out of it, then bandaged it up.

I can honestly say that I overlooked this psychosis months before. Jeremy and I had gone out to a nightclub to see Lil Wayne perform. Some guy walked past Jeremy and bumped into him. He was holding a drink in his hand, and it spilled on his shirt. He turned and said, "Excuse you!" He and the guy locked eyes. Neither one of them were going to back down, so Jeremy placed the glass on the table. I walked up to him and tried to get him to come back to the table. He walked away very angry and mumbling under his breath. The guy walked away, talking under his breath as well.

Jeremy continued to look over at the table where the other guy was sitting.

The guy stood there talking to his friends. He continued to look over at Jeremy. Jeremy got up and walked over to the table. Immediately a fight broke out in the middle of the club. While they were fighting, three of his friends jumped in to help. I tried to break it up the fight, but I was no match for the four aggressive men that were jumping him. I ran outside to get the car while they were tearing the club up.

Jeremy made it to the front door where I was waiting with the car. One of the guys came charging after him, and I put the car in drive. I came close to hitting him, but he jumped out of the way. I quickly put the car in reverse to get out of the parking lot. In the midst of backing up, I hit Lil Wayne's tour bus. They never made it off the bus to perform. The fight was too much. I had ignored too many serious warnings like this. That wasn't the first or last bar fight that he'd have.

Jeremy continued to harass me for the next few months. He would slash my tires at night, so I couldn't leave for work in the morning. I came home one afternoon from work to find my front door kicked in. I had lost my key in the midst of all of this. I had to leave the front door unlocked so that I could get in and out. When the landlord finally changed the lock, I was able to lock my doors again.

He kicked in my front door because I locked him out. He had been coming over every morning while I wasn't at home. He would sit and chill in my house all day while I was at work. He would stand next to the neighbor's garage, directly across the alley from my house. He watched who came and went. I didn't call the police or press charges because that was against the street code. The dumbest code ever! I asked Hank to come and stay for a couple of nights. He was in the process of relocating, so he didn't mind. He would stay at the house during the day while I was at work.

I couldn't change Jeremy's behavior, so I packed up my apartment and moved away. I couldn't figure out where all this insecurity came from. He had slept with both of Jasmine's best friends. One was claiming to be pregnant, and the other would creep around with him while I was at work. They loved his thug ways. He was the type of person you could hang out with in the streets then leave him with the other trash. Before I moved, I went to pick my son up from Candy's house. I didn't know that Jeremy had been staying with her. She lived about two blocks away from me. No wonder why he stalked me so conveniently. I walked in the door at Candy's house and dropped Xavier off. I noticed that Molly's car, Jasmine's friend, was parked outside. I turned around and went back in the house. Candy said that Jeremy was in the other room sleeping.

I tried to sneak in and out without seeing him, but when I saw the car sitting outside I couldn't resist. I went right to the back room where he was sleeping. He and Molly were laying on the bed talking. After all the talks about their friendship, the proof was right in front of me. I grabbed Molly and started punching her in the face. I was already done with him, but she had sat in my house for years and denied that they had been seeing each other.

We fought for about 15 minutes. She never made it off the bed to throw a punch. She laid on her back trying to kick me as I delivered punch after punch to her face. She was a sorry excuse for a friend and woman. I busted all the windows out of her car and slashed all her tires as I was leaving.

I wasn't upset about him because I didn't want him, but the mere fact that she was a family friend. Jasmine had defended their friendship, and I tried to honor that. She disrespected everything that we stood for, and I couldn't allow that.

I had shifted my focus from relationships to destiny. I was trying to find my purpose in life. My New Year's resolution when I turned 25-years old was to go back to school and buy a house. I had been in school part time for a few years. I was taking one class at a time because I had to work full time and take care of my children. I had been in school about a year before Jeremy, and I split.

In addition to all the things he had done to me, I found out that he had touched my neighbor's 12-year old daughter when we were together. She feared to tell me because she had seen the things he was capable of.

I truly contemplated killing him; child molestation was a serious offense. After hearing my struggle with sexual abuse, why wouldn't she tell me? I had to call Hank and tell him what had happened. Anytime something major went wrong he was the person I could always call.

Hank talked me down, I wanted to find Jeremy and address the issue. Whatever happened just happened, but I knew that if I went down this path, my children would be left to live the same parentless life I'd had.

I left the situation alone. I made up my mind to write Jeremy off for good. Since I moved away, I have only seen him once, and that was accidental.

Life had to go on!

Chapter 12 -
Single Living at 28-Years Old

After several years of bad relationships, I decided to be single for a while. Learning to love yourself is the most valuable learning experience of them all. When you're single, you have time to enjoy yourself. I loved the idea of marriage and happily ever after, but I hadn't found the right person to experience that with. I was in love with the concept of love. I was a hopeless romantic looking for my prince charming. I believed in the happily ever after fairy tales.

I still believe they exist, but not the tales you read in books or watch on television. Those stories are scripted and depict a false ideation of true romance or marriage. I returned to church and found my inner peace. I was at a place of rest with everything that happened. I spent the next two years trying to find myself. I learned that there wasn't anything wrong with me. I was a young, beautiful, intelligent young woman who had given her heart in the wrong way. I had to learn to love me before I could expect that from others.

Hank and I had made amends about our past and were trying to make things work. I had stipulations this time around, and he obliged. We had decided to remarry and start our life over. I had found faith and refused to live my life in the same manner as before. We chose to wait until he got out of jail to get married this time around. I refused to be in a relationship with someone that wouldn't marry me willingly. I wasn't willing to accept the concept of a jailhouse romance. I longed to be wanted of his free will. The choice had to come from a free mind, heart, and spirit. I refused to accept the notion that I was his everything because he was now incarcerated.

I wanted Hank to prove the feelings that he had expressed all these years. The day came, and we were married at our church. It was a private ceremony, witnessed by a few members of the church. His feelings came and went so quickly. He stood by his word, but his actions were quite the opposite. He had begun seeing his ex-girlfriends and hanging out all night. He was friends with members of my family, so they knew his whereabouts. Endless nights of drinking, drugs, and women. From the moment he said I do, he showed his behind. I chalked his actions up to revenge for our previous marriage. I took responsibility for ruining it, so maybe this was his way of getting me back.

I didn't know what to do with myself. I spent hours in the closet crying and praying to God for understanding. I prayed that Hank would change his wicked ways. All the people he surrounded himself with had ill intentions. They wanted to see him behave this way because he confessed that he was going to be better this time around. They knew that if he were introduced to the same lifestyle, he would revert back to his old ways. They reeled him in hook, line, and sinker. When he became too immersed in the lifestyle, they all left him high and dry.

He was having sex with both of his children's mothers, his sister's girlfriend, and countless other women. Although he and my brother Iman were friends, he didn't hide any of his indiscretions. It was clear that he wanted to make sure I hurt the same way I hurt him. I wanted to have a child and settle down, but he told me that if I had a child with him that he would also have to have one with his baby's mother. WHAT? I'm your wife! I'll be dang gone if I ever agree to something that foolish. Who did this man actually think I was? I wasn't a side chick or some random person he had met off the streets. Did he not remember all the years I had invested in him? That was the absolute last straw!

I hurtled out of control; I started popping ecstasy to ease the pain. I went to college during the day and worked in the hospital in the evening. I did everything I could to stay on track and numb the pain. I thought that I would spend the rest of my life with this man. We had been through so much, I thought that we had bypassed the hard part. We occasionally had sex from time to time, but we were no longer living together. He came over a few months later, and we popped some pills and had sex. He blindfolded me and told me to hold on.

He left the room and returned within a few minutes. He sat at the top of the bed caressing my head. I felt a touch on one of my thighs and then a moist tongue on my vagina. The texture and motion of the tongue was nothing like his. Plus, how could he be caressing my head and giving me oral sex at the same time? I immediately demanded that he untie me and remove the blindfold. I looked around the room, and there was no one there. I demanded to know who else was in the room with us. He had brought his baby's mother to my home.

She was hiding in the closet with a lingerie set on. She came out of the closet, and he began to explain. He said, "She wore her best for you. She got all dressed up to surprise you." Surprise me? We had talked adamantly about his past never crossing over into my bedroom. They were used to having sex parties, but that was long after me. He swore that he would never ask me to participate in any activity like this. They both began to plead with me. He stormed out of the room and told her to talk to me.

She sat down on the bed next to me and began telling how much we both loved him. She asked, "Why can't we share him?" I had to explain that this was against everything I believed in.

The cheating was one thing, but participating was completely another. Hank returned to the room, and I stood up and hit him as many times as I could. How could he ever violate me in this manner? He was thrown off guard because I had never put my hands on him. He became infuriated! I got dressed and dropped them both off. Hank had run out to pick her up in my car, so I had to take her home. He had it in his mind that he would have both of us. He said that he needed three weeks to make up his mind on what he wanted to do. He didn't need three weeks because my mind was made up. I changed all the locks at my home and immediately went to the courthouse and filed for a divorce.

I started dating someone else to take my mind off the last six months. I got pregnant on day number three. I had gotten off my birth control so that Hank and I could have a child. Dang it! This was not the outcome I had in mind. The condom broke, and that was the end of that story. He was young, immature, ignorant and full of drama. The second worst relationship in my life! This is the most you'll hear about that relationship.

I gave birth to son number two! He was a bright, pale, little thin boy with green eyes. I almost began to wonder if he had been switched at birth. I called him my green-eyed burrito because he loved to be wrapped tight. A month before he was born, I graduated from nursing school in May, 2005. I had my fifth child, another son, at 33-years old. He absolutely completed my family.

It was a struggle raising all these children without the help and support of their fathers. Jasmine and Zaire had moved out of state, and I had made plans to join them. At the last minute, everything fell through. I had packed my house, terminated my lease and resigned from my job. The only thing I could salvage was my job, but we became homeless. We had nowhere else to go. I placed all of my things at a friend's house and went to a hotel for the weekend. When Monday morning came, I headed for the homeless shelter.

Any government funded program establishes guidelines based on income. They encourage you to get a job and get on your feet, but they want you to do it quick and not on their dime. We were asked to leave after two weeks of being in the shelter. They said that this was a place for people that had nothing. I informed my case manager that I was already employed and just needed some time to find housing. She said as long as I was employed, I could take up residence at a hotel. We packed up our room and headed to a hotel. We bounced around from hotel to hotel for several months.

It was a daily battle to find someone to watch my three little ones. We ate fast food on a daily basis. The hotel room didn't have a kitchen area. Some days we would go to the in-laws and have a home cooked meal. I enjoyed visiting the in-laws because the kids could get out the cramped hotel room and enjoy some freedom. The boys and I would walk to the park, and they could run freely. One night I was packing the kids up to return to the hotel. The police had driven past me minutes prior to getting in the car. I didn't pay it much attention because I was concerned with getting the kids together. We pulled off and made it about a block before we were surrounded by three squad cars. I had gotten a new used minivan while at the shelter, but the plates hadn't come in yet.

They ran my driver's license, and it was suspended. I had forgotten to pay a fine. They towed the van with all of our clothing in it. I pleaded and begged with the officer to please just let someone else drive the van. I was barely holding on at this point. I had a meltdown! The stress and pressure of life had gotten to me. One more thing on top of the mountain that was already in front of me. This was our only means of transportation. If I couldn't work, I couldn't afford the hotel, food, diapers, milk or anything else. My mother-in-law came to the scene and drove us back to the hotel.

The officer took my driver's license and temporary vehicle tags. I was able to get the van towed without the tags on it. With the temporary tags being gone, I had to drive around the city without it. It was a 50-mile drive from my hotel to the job. I had to make it another week until payday to get the license plates. I owed the dealership $100 so they wouldn't release the plates to me until I paid the debt.

I sat in the parking lot of my hotel smoking a cigarette and contemplating suicide. When was I going to catch a break? I watched my three sons play with the rocks; I thought of how awful their lives would be without me. No one else worried about their safety or well-being, but me. I have promised my children I would never leave them. How could I entertain these foolish thoughts? I got myself up off the ground and brushed those thoughts away. I knew what had to be done and how to do it.

A few weeks later I found a five-bedroom house. The sign was in the yard, and the landlord was inside working on a few things. I knocked on the screen door, and he walked toward the door. He invited me to come in to see the place. I did a walk through and discussed the terms of the lease. He asked me a little bit of background information and then allowed me to fill out an application. His wife called me back the next day with an approval. I gave him $400 as a sign of good faith. He said he would hold the money as part of the deposit. I told him that I could pay the remaining balance on Friday. I was so excited that my children had a home to come to.

My two daughters had been staying with friends during this time. There wasn't much space in the hotel room, so they decided to stay with friends. I had all these people that depended on me, but absolutely no one I could depend on. All the foolish decisions I had made. I seemed to be mimicking my mother's path at times. I could never have called upon their fathers for help because they all had the same story, "You're a good mom with a good job" or "You don't need any help!"

That was an excuse to neglect their responsibilities as parents. These were the only men in the world I knew who have child support orders but have never been forced to pay. Even the strongest person needs help. I'm a very prideful person, so I'm not going to catch you down. I wasn't the one to beg for assistance. At times, I worked two or three jobs. My children couldn't go without because their fathers refused to help.

The day came that we moved into our house. I was drained from all the emotional roller coasters I had been on. It was time for a drastic change! This change meant leaving everything I knew and starting over. Like most people, change takes courage. Hank was talking about marriage, and I couldn't even entertain that thought again. I continued working hard and planning for the future.

As I was sitting at my desk, I received an email from an old friend. The email simply read, "Hey stranger." It was from Nazir. He was deployed in the Middle East, and he wanted to talk. My heart was beating with excitement! I hadn't talked to him for a few years. We had spoken periodically throughout the years. He had enlisted in the military and moved across the world. He had gotten married and had children. We always stayed connected through social media, but rarely did we speak on the phone.

In our last conversation, we had discussed meeting out of state. He was at school doing some formal training for his career. When I separate from people I typically cut ties, but this had been different. We had parted ways, but we always checked in to see how life had been treating one another. I didn't feel anyone should have access to me once we separated. There are no such things as "only friends" when you have as much history as the two of us. I had a deep dark secret that needed to come out. I had held this secret for many years, and only three people knew.

Nazir called me three weeks after my second child was born. He asked if he was the father of my child. We had parted ways when I first got pregnant with my second child. I didn't want to hold him back from the future he deserved, so I said: "NO." You remember I told you that Hank was not the father. Nazir was. Hank and I continued the relationship knowing the details of my pregnancy. When my daughter turned 13-years old I tried to talk to her and Hank about the situation. She said she really didn't want to know about her father. Hank said that he didn't think that the conversation needed to be revisited.

He never wanted to know the truth; Ria was his daughter, and nothing could change that. He had raised her all these years, and it wouldn't make a difference. Jasmine had known since the beginning, and she never let me forget. I couldn't keep this secret any longer, so I told Nazir. His response was, "Doesn't she have a father?" He questioned why I wanted to tell her at this point. Hank said that she was his little girl.

I let the situation die down again, but when she turned 17-years old, I told everyone the truth. Nazir said that he would find a way for us to do an official DNA test. Nazir wanted to develop a relationship with Ria but questioned whether it was the right time.

Ria has an introverted personality, soft spoken voice, and calm spirit. She was more like her father than I had ever known. I always wondered where her nature came from. Nazir and Ria exchanged numbers and began to develop a relationship. They took things one day at a time.

Nazir returned stateside a few months later. Upon his return, Nazir and I spoke about the DNA testing. He instructed me to go to a store and gather a home collection kit. The sample could be collected at home and sent to an official lab for testing.

The lab would supply certified documentation to be used in court. I swabbed Ria's and my mouth and packaged the sample. I sent the sample to Nazir for his DNA collection. The DNA processing took close to three weeks for the results. That seemed to be a long three weeks.

Nazir and I talked on the phone from time to time. Our conversation was more frequent than it had ever been. He was separated from his wife, and I was single. I always treated my birthday like a national holiday. I enjoyed traveling so this was usually the time of year I got to do it.

My 35th birthday was approaching, and I wanted to do something special. I had a deep burning passion to visit New York. Nazir had spent part of his childhood in Brooklyn, so I asked if he would be my tour guide. He agreed to accompany me on my trip, but he couldn't be my tour guide. He quickly reminded me that he had no prior knowledge of his living experience in Brooklyn. He needed a global positioning system to get around the city he currently lived in.

We settled on a weekend in NY, NY in Las Vegas instead. We planned our trip over the next few weeks. I was nervous to actually see him face to face after all these years; my excitement grew as the time neared.

Chapter 13 -
The Truth Shall Make You Fear

I jumped on a bus and headed to work pulling my large luggage bag behind me. I was going to work half a day, then head to the airport to catch my flight. I got off work and ran through the lunch hour crowd. I was moving down the street as fast as I could. The bus was approaching, and I was a half a block away from the stop. I hurried to the bus headed downtown where I would then transfer to a train that would take me to the airport. I arrived at the packed airport. The airport was full of people traveling to various parts of the world. I stood in the middle of the airport reading all the signs. All of these airplanes parked at the gates, ready to fly anywhere in the world. My world seemed so small to me at this moment. I picked up my cell phone and called Nazir.

I wanted to make sure that he was able to get out of his mandatory training early. He had discussed the details of our trip with his supervisor, but I still wanted to check in. He had assured me that he would be able to make it. He didn't answer so I left him a message on his cell phone. He was away from his office so I knew he couldn't be reached there. Even if he didn't make it, this would be an experience of its own.

I approached the counter to collect my boarding passes. The attendant assured me that my flight was leaving on time. Las Vegas was about a two-and-a-half-hour flight. As we flew over the city of LV, the whole city was lit up. Every hotel displays a unique attraction. The colors are so bright that they can be seen throughout the sky. It was the most beautiful thing that I had ever seen. I arrived at the airport and took a shuttle to my hotel. I was tired from the anticipation, so I decided to take a nap once I checked in.

I hadn't received a text or call from Nazir, so I waited. I slept for about two hours before I heard a knock on the door. I opened the door and there stood my high school sweetheart! High school had been a lifetime ago, but he had changed. He looked like a mature version of himself. He still maintained his youth and unique style of dress. We both stood in the door speechless. We had come on this trip as two friends.

I laid back down, and he sat in the chair. The excitement had turned into an awkward moment. I began to question whether we had made a huge mistake or not. I got up and started to get dressed. We weren't going to waste this trip just sitting in the hotel room. We began the night with some basic conversation and shyness, but at the end of the night, we were old friends. We went to a club and had a few drinks. He was the type of gentleman that took you out and treated you like a lady. He opened doors and paid the tabs. I couldn't remember the last time someone paid a tab. The feelings and memories came rushing back. We ended the night at an old NY pizzeria inside the hotel.

That morning he got up and said that he'd return. He returned with coffee for the two of us. He was the sweetest guy I had ever met. He was so thoughtful and caring. It seemed as though we were connecting from where we left off. These were the things that I loved about him as a young girl. I wasn't ready for a mature relationship of this magnitude when I was a 16-year old; I hadn't dealt with the enemies inside of me. We purchased tickets to several attractions that day. We walked around holding hands like a high school couple, laughing and giggling while enjoying life. We walked down the strip, in and out of shops. A salesman approached us and asked if we wanted to attend a presentation. He said that we had to be married in order to qualify. The salesperson took us upstairs, and we picked out matching wedding rings. We looked at each other as if it was a sign. A sign that we were supposed to be here in this moment. After the presentation, we returned to the hotel room.

We kept the rings on for several weeks after our trip. We laid in bed and discussed the "what ifs" of our relationship. What if we would have gotten married? What if we would have moved away together? What if we were still together? These were not questions that could be answered, he had a past, and so did I. I was a broken hearted girl from the streets, and he was a guy that had traveled the world.

Our world experiences didn't align anywhere. How could we make this work? Nazir always wanted to be a protector of the women in his life. He wanted to be a husband and a provider for our family, but I wasn't in the place to allow him to do so. I didn't love myself, so how could I expect him to love me? I was so blind by my past that I couldn't see my future. We both had our own issues to work out. We had both been previously married and had children from those marriages.

We fell asleep with the thoughts of yesterday on our minds. The early morning came quickly; our alarms were sounding as our weekend came to an end. We knew that we both had to get back to the reality of our lives. We packed up our things and headed to the airport. We shared a cab to the airport. We cuddled and held hands as we drove away from the city. My heart had a new beat. When we reconnected, all the feelings of the past exploded. We bubbled with the love we had once felt.

Our talks on the phone and text messages to each other were nonstop. We talked from the time we woke up until we fell asleep again. We had so much to catch up on. I could talk for hours, and he would listen. We couldn't wait to be in each other's arms again. The people at work noticed a change in me. They wanted to know where this man came from, where I met him and how our weekend went. I have never really talked about him in the past. Only my family and close friends knew of him from our childhood. We spent early mornings on the phone, we talked straight through lunch and again at bedtime. People quickly began to take notice.

I planned a trip to his home; this time I was searching for a future. I wanted to know if this was more than a weekend romance. I left the children with various family members for two weeks. I arranged for everyone to pitch in with their care. That was a complete nightmare for me. I couldn't bring them because they had to attend school, plus, I didn't know how this man lived. I had to take this trip to explore things for myself

I wanted to get out and see the city of Oceanside, California, investigate the job market, and consider the housing market. It was a beautiful city on the coast of California. On a summer day, it could be 90 degrees with a cool ocean breeze. I could feel the bright, crisp sunshine beat on my face as I stepped outside. We went on a different date each night. We enjoyed dinner on the beach, walks in the park, amusement parks and so much more. I got a chance to see how he had been living life the last few decades. I didn't tell him, but I had made up my mind. I was ready to step out on faith and make a complete change.

Friday finally came, and I had him all to myself. He had been working during the day and entertaining me at night. He got off work early so we could take a train to San Diego and flew to the Dominican Republic. Our resort was next to the beach. Nazir and I woke up to a sunrise full of color. It was an array of colors; the reds and oranges glistening off the bright blue water. The water was so clear that you could look down and see the fish as they swam around my feet. The smell of the salt in the air was so freshening.

The sound of the waves as they hit the sand and retreated back to the ocean. My life now seemed like the ocean; a sea of endless possibilities. The depth and magnitude of its greatness cannot be explained. It represents the marvelous nature of God; the more you seek Him, the more there is to receive. Our smallest thoughts and dreams can never be compared to His awesomeness.

We spent the weekend hanging out and talking. Before we realized, it was time to head home. We walked and explored every inch of the city. The people, the fun, and the scenery. I realized that this was where I wanted to be. I had wanted to change the people that I had surrounded myself with for so many years. I had never lived away from my family, and now I was contemplating moving to the other side of the country. I was the oldest sibling, and they depended on me for stability.

Nazir was always a great man. He had always loved me in the way I deserved to be loved. He was raised by a single parent, but he didn't view women the same as the other men I had dated. I guess when I look back over my relationship trends, I dated men who were raised by single parents. A parent had left them with a void. We had the same common denominator; we were all missing a parent. That void of knowing who we were or where we came from spilled over into our relationships and parenting styles.

We jumped on the train heading to Oceanside. When we arrived, we were greeted by an angry father. Nazir had failed to communicate to his father that we were heading home. He was furious with us, and I didn't know why there was so much hostility. I wasn't the one responsible for communicating our whereabouts. He told Nazir that he had sat around all day waiting for him to call. He had neglected to inform him when our train would arrive. This made for an awkward car ride home. I wasn't going to let the negativity ruin our last night together, so I apologized to him for the inconvenience. I thanked him for taking the time to pick us up from the train station. We were high off life, so nothing was going to ruin the great weekend we had just experienced.

We got back to the house and went directly to Nazir's room. We made passionate love all night and then he held me in his arms until the sun came up. I remember thinking, please don't ever let me go.

Chapter 14 -
The DNA Bombshell!

Monday morning, Nazir got dressed and headed to work. He reentered the house with a hand full of mail. He dropped the pile of mail on the counter and left out for work. The letters fell in a fan position. I was sitting at the counter being nosey, as usual, and I noticed an envelope addressed to him from the testing lab. I opened the letter, and it read the legal jargon about Nazir being a 99.9% probability of being Ria's father. I opened the computer to check my email for results. I had received my copy of the DNA test results as well.

I studied each chromosome by chromosome, line by line to the end. I wanted to make sure that I was reading the information correctly before I picked up the phone to call Nazir. The information was 99.9% correct! I called Nazir at work; he wasn't in the office, so I left him a message to call me back. He called me back within a few minutes. I read him the results over the phone. He was still a little quite unsure, so I called the lab's customer service center on a conference call. He asked the woman to interpret the results, and she said: "You're the father." He was quiet at first, so I didn't know what to think. I asked him if he needed a minute to process the information, but he said that he was fine! He was now the proud father of an 18-year old daughter.

The DNA bombshell went off like a nuclear bomb inside our families. I had just pissed every in-law I could think of off! I called Hank to let him know what the results said. Hank actually took the news the worst. We argued for several weeks following the results. He called me every name in the book. I couldn't believe his reaction.

He was one of the three people that knew all these years. We thought that we had made the best decision, for our family, at that time. Nazir had gotten married and started a family of his own, and I had moved on with my life. In my mind, it didn't matter if I told him. I would have never let my daughter go out of the state, let alone the country. That was just more motivation to keep the information to myself.

I was "raised" in a single parent home, how hard could it be to raise my own? There was a brief period when we had a two-parent household. I didn't see the benefit in that as I got older. I watched my stepfather, Clay, beat my mother on more than one occasion. Who needs a two-parent household if this was her reality? My stepfather taught me some very important life lessons. The first was, *Live outside the box because you never have to settle for ordinary.* The second was, never allow anyone to abuse you.

He hadn't lived up to his own advice. You cannot say that you love someone, then turn around and misuse them. His actions spoke louder than his words. I hated him for what he had done to Annie for so many years. I hated the weak person that she had become. It took me many years to realize that it wasn't entirely his fault. He was abusive, and there's no excuse for that, but she had to be the one to stop him.

A man should never put his hands on a woman. The person she became was on her. She had to accept responsibility for her own actions. Her actions impacted her life, and now I had let mine do the same. My daughter had lost 18 years with her father, and they didn't deserve that. It was time to make amends with my past.

Hank couldn't understand why I was rehashing old issues. Defending myself from every attack that came my way. I tried to explain that regardless of how we felt this was the best decision at the time. There were other lives that were involved in our decision, and they deserved to know the truth.

Hank and his family hurled insult after insult; there would be irreversible damage behind this. I also had to deal with Nazir's family. You see, it didn't matter what role Hank played in the relationship, but when I hurt him, the world came to a complete halt. Although we were pretending to be friends, I always made sure he was okay. The truth was, I couldn't stay in this type of dysfunctional relationship for the rest of my life.

Hank was in multiple relationships, but when I mentioned to him that I was moving away he was hurt. Hurt for what? Because I have chosen to move on with my life and let you be who you are? I couldn't be in a relationship with someone that couldn't be honest with themselves. He was engaged to a stripper and dating a woman that was mentally ill. I tried to discuss the possibilities of a future, but I knew deep down inside he could never be the man I needed him to be. He said that he owed a debt to one of the women and he couldn't let her go. I wasn't heart-broken but relieved that we had finally come to the same consensus. He needed his somebody, and I needed Nazir.

I had to clean up my mess and move on. I had dysfunctional people all around me. How could I heal or move on if I never gave myself the opportunity to? I needed to force myself to let go of the past and move forward.

I returned from my trip late in February. We decided that I'd move to California, come June, when the children got out of school. June seemed like it was years away. I asked Tierra and Ria if they wanted to make the big move to California with me. Tierra was 19-years old. Our relationship hadn't always been close. Honestly, we struggled to be around each other.

Tierra was the child that made my life very difficult. We had two physical altercations since she was 16-years old. She had to be kicked out for a few months then I allowed her to come home. Our cohesiveness was always short lived. I always wanted the relationship with her that I didn't have with my mother.

Our personalities had very similar traits, and that added an additional strain on our bond. Tierra was always stubborn and independent. I didn't have a problem allowing her to grow and learn, but she constantly challenged me.

She said that she was going to stay and finish high school. She had dropped out for about a year. She chose an alternative program that she enjoyed. She had her mind set on graduating, and I wanted to assist her in any way that I could. Tierra decided that she was going to stay with some of her friends. I didn't object.

Ria had a difficult decision to make as well. She has a nine-month old baby boy. She was still involved with his father. It took her a while to decide if she was coming. She initially said no, but as time neared, she changed her mind.

Xavier was 11-years old, D.J. was five-years-old, and C.J. was two-years-old. Xavier hadn't seen Jeremy in years. We separated when he was about three-years-old. He didn't understand why his father didn't want to be a part of his life. I tried to explain that he wasn't the issue. His father was a nasty, abusive man and I didn't want him around him. I had allowed him to spend the night at Jeremy's house a few times, but the last time I picked him up, he was full of urine.

Xavier was a bed wetter, and he didn't take the proper hygiene steps to keeping himself clean. Jeremy was a poor father that neglected to do anything for him.

D.J. was very close to his father, Sean. They were almost twins. He didn't understand what the move meant for their relationship. D.J. was already taking the separation hard. C.J. was too young to understand any of it.

I instructed everyone on what needed to be done before we could leave. I couldn't take all of my furniture with me, so I had to liquidate as much of it as possible.

Over the next few months, I began downsizing my house. Nazir had a fully furnished house, and I couldn't bring all my things with me. I sold everything in my home except the kid's bunk beds, their bikes and a few totes of our clothes. We packed everything we could fit in the back of a U-Haul. At first, I was anxious about selling everything. I didn't want to feel as if I had nothing. These were material possessions; everything you lose can be regained. The true strength was leaving everything and starting fresh!

The day before Mother's Day, I went and picked up my U-Haul. I couldn't wait until June. It had been 20 plus years since we had been together and I was ready for a change. I packed up the U-Haul within an hour or two. I had moved the date up, so my family was in shock. We went out for our final dinner, and we sailed off. My daughter and I were looking forward to the new journey.

It was time for me to make my own amends!

Nazir and Ria met one week before her 18th birthday. He had stayed up all night long waiting for us to arrive. The DNA information changed many of my relationships. Nazir and I had grown closer, but others had cut off all communication with me. I took the time to say my goodbyes to those that were available. I left many close friends and family members behind. Ria was anxious because she had never met Nazir, they had only spoken on the phone. He made it his mission to build a relationship with her.

We pulled up to Nazir's home in the middle of the day. The street was empty, and all the neighbors seemed to be gone. Nazir wasn't home when we arrived. He had left for work, and his children were at school. We went into the house and began settling in. The kids were anxious to meet Nazir. They had heard so much about him, and they didn't know what to expect. I walked into his bedroom to find a bundle of flowers and a box of chocolates on the bed. Nazir had made up the extra bedroom for Ria. She found flowers and candy on her bed as well.

Nazir typically got off work about 5:00 p.m., headed to get his children from school, then came home. He walked into the house with the biggest grin on his face. Ria was a little apprehensive about greeting him. I chuckled as they slowly hugged each other. They were peas in a pod from the moment they met. They had similar personalities.

They were both quiet and reserved individuals. They were both introverts, the kind that needs information dragged out of them. We all spent the first few days getting to know one another. While Nazir was at work, we explored our new city. They slowly came around and opened up to one another. They hadn't even realized how close they had become. The awkwardness was over, and we could begin the rest of our lives. I was in heaven and loving every bit of my freedom.

Chapter 15 -
Reflections of My Teenage Self

As I looked over my life, it mirrored that of my mother's. I had always despised the way that she raised us, but I realized that some of those things that I despised carried over to my own parenting. I found myself in some of the very same situations as Annie. I had to look in the mirror and fix me. I see the patterns of instability, the trail of broken relationships and the same disconnect from my oldest daughter.

A woman's ideation, thoughts, beliefs, and values about a man come from her father. In today's society, men seem to lack the understanding of their position in the home. Growing up, I heard all kinds of things about my biological father's character, his behavior, and his absence. The earliest memories of him were of him taking care of Jasmine and me at my grandparent's home. I spoke to my aunt about the recollection of these memories, and she asked how I could remember this. She said I was too young then. I believe my recollection was tied to trauma. Jasmine used to terrorize me with this large black spider.

I was a young, timid child. The instability of my parents directly influenced my foundation. I have a vivid memory of Annie leaving out to call the police. She said that Imus had started the house on fire and she needed assistance.

For years, I argued the details of this scenario with my grandmother. She said, "Nyla that's not the truth." She always approached each situation with compassion and empathy.

I said, "Grandma that's your son, of course, you're going to defend him!" The man that she knew and raised was not the man that had been portrayed to me all these years.

He has his issues like any other man, but he wasn't the type of man to abandon his children. Through the years, he could never make contact with us because we hadn't been anywhere long enough. He was the last person that Annie would ever attempt to contact.

I grew up wondering how my father could just leave his children. How could a man burn down the home that his children resided in? Years went by before we reconciled the differences in that story. My foundation of abandonment was formulated at a very young age.

Imus wasn't a saint, he had another child that was six months older than me. Annie had this ideation that if a man had other children, they weren't your siblings. She didn't believe in half-siblings, so we had a distant relationship with our sister. We grew up disowning her because her mother and my mother didn't get along. There were more lies formed between the two of these women.

Unimaginable lies that shook the foundation of our souls. My father had his share of relationships, but rapist was something that he wasn't. One child grew up believing that she was a product of rape, another believing that he was an arsonist, and the last believing that she didn't belong to him. Two women fighting over one man and both ended up without him. Instead of either woman telling their children the truth, they allowed them to live a lie.

My sister was conceived consensually, but when the truth of her mother's actions showed itself through pregnancy out of wedlock, her mother lied to hide her shame. She lied and said that she was raped by my father. She defamed my father's character in order to save her own. It sounds better to be the victim rather than letting the truth be heard. She was imperfect and made a mistake by having sex before marriage.

That was something that any parent that truly loves their child could overcome. You don't put the burden of truth on your child or another person to maintain self. The root of this problem is pride first, then shame and guilt. You don't have to live in the lies of your past. Pride occurs when you refuse to seek God's ways and God's word. Own your mistakes and make amends with your past. You're hiding behind your pride and dishonoring the truth.

Pride has detrimental effects on our lives. Hurt and pain turn into bitterness; bitterness governs your life. People that truly love you will be honest and tell you the truth. We have to get out from under the lies that we bury ourselves in. I wrote this book to help someone in need. We all need forgiveness, wisdom, and guidance.

I chose men that didn't have high expectations. I didn't have to push myself to deal with my past because they didn't challenge me to become a better me. I could hide the person I was and the things that had happened to me. I didn't realize then, but I fully understand now, my shame controlled my every decision. I inflicted more hurt and pain on myself because I refused to deal with my past.

Unleashing my secret brought me great peace. There is no such thing as reputation in the eyes of God. The truth is the truth, regardless of how it affects people.

Years went by, and Annie maintained the same story about Imus. It didn't matter how long it had been, it just didn't sit right with me. We were having Sunday dinner at Clay's house. Although he and Annie didn't work out, they maintained a civilized relationship over the years. The three of us were sitting at the table, and I confronted Annie and Clay.

Clay scratched his head and said, "Baby." He didn't need to say anymore. I dropped my head with great disappointment. I knew what followed after that was not going to be the story I had heard all these years. Clay told me that they had lied about Imus. He was honest with his explanation of his involvement and how it played out. I couldn't believe that they had lied all these years. I despised them at first, but then let it go. I felt the need to rectify my relationship with Imus.

The initial hurt and injury were hard. I knew that my grandmother didn't have any need to lie to me. I wanted to believe Annie because she was my mother. She was the one that was responsible for my existence. No matter how rough our lives were, she was there dragging us through it.

I called Imus the very next morning. I sat in my car outside the library and poured my heart out. I had to make amends with the information I had lived by. Our relationship didn't start off close, but it grew quickly. We began talking on the phone almost every day. We had hashed out all the lies that had been between us.

We agreed that we'd make every effort in restoring our relationship. Imus wasn't faultless in his absence, and that's something that he'll have to deal with. We've tried to bond over the years, but I guess old habits are hard to break. He's so busy pretending to be the man that he's neglected to be a man for his children. I now know that we moved from place to place and state to state. How could a person battling their own issues keep up with us?

There was a very real time when this would have affected me, but I am content with my life. I no longer look for a father figure in my life.

As parents, it's all too common to disconnect from that someone we've had children with once the relationship is over. The children become causalities of war. In the wake of the devastation, we remember that there are innocent little ones trying to grasp what happened with their absent parent. We run from our pain and lie to protect ourselves from the truth.

Parents make decisions that impact their children for the rest of their lives. As children, we don't understand the extent of it all, but as we grow and mature it is our duty to seek the truth. Just because you have lived a lie for years doesn't mean you can't rectify it with the truth. It is honestly not fair to the other parent, the child, or yourself.

You can always look at other people and blame them for your life decisions. I had just as much responsibility as the people that I allowed in my life. The warning signs were always there, but I ignored them. In the midst of the worst situation, I decided to stay when I knew I should have left. Part of living life is to accept responsibility and making amends with your past. No one human being is perfect; we accept when we're wrong.

I couldn't blame all of my life issues on the things that happened in my past. Some of the bad things that occurred were truly out of my control, and others I was the root cause. It's taken me years to deal with my inner me. I had to peel back the layers of self-centeredness, anger, and rage before I could learn who I was. I was so angry with my father for years.

Nazir suggested that we go to therapy years ago. I was hesitant at first, like most, but when I went, I discovered some hidden issues. I had more anger toward my father for abandoning me than I did at Ben for molesting me. I felt that if my father hadn't left then, none of this would have ever happened. That was completely untrue! I have worked through those feelings. Those raw emotions were keeping me from being a decent human being. I looked at all men with the same contempt.

Nazir was not responsible for any of the things that happened in my past. Why should he be held accountable for it? I couldn't love me because I didn't know who I was. I identified myself as a girl with low self-esteem, then a protective mother. That wasn't the real me. Those were roles that I had taken on.

All this pain had to have a purpose. I bottled up my negative emotions and used them to build a bridge to my destiny. Pain has its purpose, but don't let it consume you. Learn who you are! What your destiny is! What plans and purpose is meant for your life? It took me many years to love the woman deep down inside of me.

She had been broken and mistreated for so long that she didn't believe that she deserved love. I look at life through a new lens, I know that I would never accept the things that I once allowed. I also wouldn't treat others in that manner. Nazir dealt with my worst, and now he has my best.

I got up out of that cold, dead grave and dusted myself off. I walked away from that empty shell and straight into my destiny!

I graduated with my bachelor's degree in Nursing in 2015. I am currently seeking my Master's degree in nursing.

I have also begun the process of starting a non-profit girls' home called Extended Blessings. My dream is to provide a home (Faith Place) for young women with children. Juvenile Horizons shaped my future forever, and I want to provide that same experience to other young women in my situation.

Extended Blessings- Hope House is my dream for young men that come from broken homes. I have met many broken young men along my journey. These young men would benefit from positive interactions with strong role models.

I look back over my journey and smile now because I MADE IT! There is Purpose in your Pain!

Extended Blessings Introduction....

Here are some true facts about the homeless youth, teenage pregnancy, and neglect or abuse. Growing up I experienced each of these phenomena's. My goal is to create awareness so that some little girl or boy doesn't have to experience these things. I have founded a home called **Extended Blessings**. Our mission is to help young women and men, ages 17-24 years old, transition through their circumstances and become productive pillars of their community. A portion of the proceeds will go toward funding this establishment. The rate of teenage pregnancy or abortion has significantly decreased over the last few decades. The number of homeless or runaway youth has decreased as well. There is still such a long way to go to improve our community and those in need.

(1) "Homeless youth" means a person 24 years of age or younger who is unaccompanied by a parent or guardian and is without shelter where appropriate care and supervision are available, whose parent or legal guardian is unable or unwilling to provide shelter and care, or who lacks a fixed, regular, and adequate nighttime residence. The following are not fixed, regular, or adequate nighttime residences."

"Youth at risk of homelessness" means a person 24 years of age or younger whose status or circumstances indicate a significant danger of experiencing homelessness in the near future. Status or circumstances that indicate a significant danger may include: (1) youth exiting out-of-home placements; (2) youth who previously were homeless; (3) youth whose parents or primary caregivers are or were previously homeless; (4) youth who are exposed to abuse and neglect in their homes; (5) youth who experience conflict with parents due to chemical or alcohol dependency, mental health disabilities, or other disabilities; and (6) runaways.

Of all births to females under 20 years of age, percent outside of marriage (no marital), 2010 **RH3**		
Total	**Minnesota**	**United States**
Females under 20 years of age	93%	88%

Females aged	**Minnesota**	**United States**
Under 15	100%	99%
15-17	97%	95%
18-19	92%	85%
15-19	93%	88%

Females aged	Minnesota	United States
Under 15	100%	99%
15-17	97%	95%

Of all births to females under 20 years of age, percent by race/ethnicity, 2010 RH3	
Mother's race/ethnicity[1]	**United States**
Non-Hispanic white	39%
Non-Hispanic black	24%
American Indian or Alaska Native[2,3]	2%
Asian or Pacific Islander[2,3]	2%
Hispanic[4]	33%

[1] Includes all births, including those with Hispanic origin not stated and not shown below. Unknown race of mother is imputed.

[2] Race and Hispanic origin are reported separately on birth certificates. Persons of Hispanic origin may be of any race. Race categories are consistent with the 1977 Office of Management and Budget (OMB) standards.

[3] Includes persons of Hispanic origin according to mother's reported race.

[4] Includes all persons of Hispanic origin of any race.

Teen pregnancy rate (pregnancies per 1,000 females aged 15-19), 2005 RH2		
Total	**Minnesota**	**United States**
Females aged 15-19	43	70

Females aged	**Minnesota**	**United States**
15-17	21	38
18-19	75	118

Percent change in the teen pregnancy rate, 1988-2005 RH2		
Total	**Minnesota**	**United States**
Change in rate to females aged 15-19 (1988 to 2005)	-38%	-37%

The teen pregnancy rate was 69 pregnancies per 1,000 females aged 15-19 in Minnesota in 1988, and 111 in the U.S. The U.S. teen pregnancy rate peaked in 1990 at 116.9 pregnancies per 1,000 females aged 15-19, but state data are not available for that year.

Teen abortion rate (abortions per 1,000 females aged 15-19), 2005 **RH2**		
Total	**Minnesota**	**United States**
Females aged 15-19	11	19

Percent change in the teen abortion rate, 1988-2005 **RH2**		
Total	**Minnesota**	**United States**
Change in rate to females aged 15-19 (1988 to 2005)	-62%	-56%

The U.S. teen abortion rate peaked at 43.5 abortions per 1,000 females aged 15-19 in 1988. The teen abortion rate for Minnesota was 29 abortions per 1,000 females aged 15-19 in 1988.

References

The Office of the Revisor of Statutes. (2016). 2015 Minnesota Statutes 256K.45 HOMELESS YOUTH ACT. Retrieved from: https://www.revisor.mn.gov/statutes/?id=256k.45 September 12, 2016.

RH3 Pregnancy and abortion rate data are from: Guttmacher Institute. (2010). U.S. teenage pregnancies, births and abortions: National and state trends and trends by race and ethnicity. Washington, DC: Guttmacher Institute. Retrieved September 12, 2016, from http://www.guttmacher.org/pubs/USTPtrends.pdf

RH2 2010 Birth data are from: Centers for Disease Control and Prevention. National Center for Health Statistics. Vital Stats. Retrieved September 12, 2016, from http://205.207.175.93/vitalstats/ReportFolders/reportFolders.aspx

Donita J. Clark was born in Wooster, Ohio and raised on the streets of Minneapolis, Minnesota. She went to high school in North Minneapolis. Donita grew up a troubled teen. She had her first child when she was only 14 years old. By the time that she turned 17 years old she had given birth to her second daughter. With two children to raise, no support system, she turned to the streets. She lived a life of crime until she finally realized her calling; or so she thought. She went back to school and obtained her G.E.D. at 19 years old. She had an overwhelming love of math, so she began her college studies as an accountant. She quickly realized that her outgoing personality did not aligned with this career path.

After years of searching, she finally found her calling in nursing. She obtained a her first nursing diploma at Saint Paul College as an LPN. She knew that she wanted to continue her education, so she attended, the Century Community College for her Registered Nurse's degree, (Associate), and then Grand Canyon University (Bachelor). She has spent the last 20 years in the healthcare field. Her drive and motivation, as a Registered Nurse, community activist and steward, comes from the desire to help others.

Donita is a wife and mother of 7 children, three girls and four boys, in total. 5 of the children are biological and the other 2 were gifted through marriage.

Donita, the Author, has just written her first book titled- *In Pain On Purpose: A world of hurt can change your destiny.* In Pain on Purpose was inspired by real events in her life. The book was written as a inspirational piece to overcoming self-hate. Nyla, the main character, endured abandonment, abuse, homelessness and then happiness. Her story is meant to encourage and inspire someone that may need a word. Someone that is struggling with their purpose or someone that has no ideal what to do with their pain. If this story can reach just one young women or man that believes all hope is gone, her goal has been accomplished. You are not alone in your struggles. Donita's life work has just begun.... Her story will take you through an emotional ride of tragedy, suspense, triumph and romance.